Hidden CHILD

An award-winning author, Anne Cassidy has written over twenty books for teenagers. She is fascinated by the way ordinary people can be sucked into crime and forced to make agonizing moral decisions.

Praise for Anne Cassidy's books:

"Totally gripping" *Books for Keeps*

"Dark, chilling and clever . . . Anne Cassidy reminds me of Minette Walters or Ruth Rendell" Celia Rees

"Always compelling" *Telegraph*

"Compassionate and unflinching" *Guardian*, Jan Mark

Hidden CHILD

anne cassidy

SCHOLASTIC

First published in the UK in 1997 by Scholastic Children's Books
An imprint of Scholastic Ltd
Euston House, 24 Eversholt Street
London, NW1 1DB, UK
Registered office: Westfield Road, Southam, Warwickshire, CV47 0RA
SCHOLASTIC and associated logos are trademarks and or registered
trademarks of Scholastic Inc.

This edition published in the UK by Scholastic Ltd, 2007
Text copyright © Anne Cassidy, 1997
The right of Anne Cassidy to be identified as the author of this work
has been asserted by her.
Cover illustration copyright © Getty Images

10 digit ISBN 0 439 95002 3
13 digit ISBN 978 0439 95002 2

British Library Cataloguing-in-Publication Data.
A CIP catalogue record for this book is available from the British Library

Printed and bound by CPI Bookmarque, Croydon, Surrey
Papers used by Scholastic Children's Books are made from wood grown
in sustainable forests.

3 5 7 9 10 8 6 4 2

www.scholastic.co.uk/zone

PART ONE

ONE

Lou had always known that her mother, Anna, was a thief.

Was *thief* too strong a word to use?

She used to think so.

When she was younger, much younger, it had been small things: toilet rolls from public conveniences, fistfuls of paper napkins from McDonald's, salt and pepper sachets from cafeterias, paper and pens from the various offices that she had worked in.

It's not really *stealing*, Anna had said. People *expect* you to take these things.

Once, Lou had been with her when someone had actually come up in front of them and called Anna a thief to her face. "THIEF! THIEF! THIEF!" she had shouted and Anna had pulled Lou away and walked hurriedly across the street, her eyes staring straight ahead as if she had been walking on a tightrope.

Anna had said that the woman was mad but Lou had known it was to do with her latest boyfriend, a tall thin man called Den who had an old sports car and a faded leather jacket that he wore all the time.

Then there were the plants: cuttings from park displays and once, after telling the gardener that someone was looking for him, even a small rose bush that was being dug up. A thorn had pierced her thumb and Lou had watched a small glass bead of blood form on Anna's skin.

It was going to be thrown out anyway, she had said.

You can't steal from *nature*, Anna had said.

I only take things that no one will miss, she had said and Lou remembered her using her fingers as a comb for the front of her hair and bending down to kiss her wetly on the forehead, the scent of her perfume sudden and heavy. Then when she stood up again it was gone, escaping into the air around her.

It wasn't true, though. Anna hadn't only taken things that no one would miss.

Stealing: taking things that belonged to other people. Had it become a way of life to her? That was what Lou fretted over.

That evening at the fair when the man in the raincoat chased them. Her thirteenth birthday. Two years before they moved to London.

It was a spring night. The day had been brilliantly sunny but the evening air felt saturated with cold. Lou was wearing a thin blouse and jeans. Underneath it was a pale peach satin bra. A present for her birthday. There were matching knickers too but she'd left them in the drawer at home. The sharp air seemed to prod through the thin fabrics, making the goosebumps rise on her skin.

Anna shivered. "So much for the spring," she said, hugging Lou with her arm.

"Oh Mum!" Lou said, disengaging herself. If the girls

from school were around they might laugh to see her mum embracing her so publicly.

"*Oh Mum! Oh Mum!*" Anna said, laughing. "What has it come to when my own daughter's embarrassed to be with me?"

"I'm not, it's just that. . ." How could Lou explain? Anna just wasn't like all the other mums that Lou had known. The girls she knew rarely went out with their mothers; only occasionally would she see them slouching along behind them in the shopping centre, rolling their eyes at things that were said. The women themselves seemed to be weary, their movements slow and cumbersome, their mouths constantly pinched as though in perpetual disapproval.

Anna was different. When she came up to school on parents' evenings she was like a big sister, not just because she looked younger, but the way she walked, the way she nudged Lou when they saw a funny-looking teacher, the way she giggled under her breath at the things that teachers said.

"Race you to the fair," Anna whispered, and Lou looked across the common at the distant caravans and carousels and juggernauts, all parked at odd angles, their lights twinkling like distant Christmas decorations. It shouldn't really be called a *fair*. It was only a tatty collection of rides and stalls – Lou had been before. It wasn't Disneyland, she was certain of that.

"One, two, three. . ." and Anna sped off ahead while Lou broke into a half-hearted trot behind her, pulling gently at the satin bra which started to rise as she ran. Anna got there first, bending over to catch her breath while Lou jogged up to her, carefully looking round to make sure no one from school was there.

Moments later they were submerged in the noise and the movement of the fair. There seemed to be thousands of people. Faces ebbed and flowed around them, their skins lit up with the blues, reds and green from the coloured lanterns. The thumping noise of the machinery underneath the tinny sound of the pop records filled Lou's head and meant that she had to mouth her words to Anna. The lights and the people created a warmth, though, and Lou stopped feeling cold as she and Anna linked arms and were swept along, in and around the rides and past the side-shows.

They didn't see the man with the raincoat then, not straight away.

They went from ride to ride: the carousel with the frozen horses, the wurlitzer, the dodgem cars, the ghost train. She'd ridden them all the year before with friends, shrieking and laughing, her hair blowing into her eyes and into the corners of her mouth. But when Anna asked if she wanted to go on them she said, "Honestly! No!" She was too grown up now to go on the rides with a parent, with her *mum*.

So they bought chips and a drink and found a step to sit on, away from the rides, near the caravans and buses that the fair people owned. Anna was singing along with a song that was playing close by. She sang the words expertly but when she put a chip into her mouth she just ummed.

"Look at the length of this," Anna shouted, holding a long chip in the air and studying it for a moment.

Lou looked at Anna's tray of chips. There were four plastic forks lying around the edge and on the ground she noticed a handful of salt sachets. Why didn't she just take what she needed? She was like a squirrel, tucking things away in case they ever needed them in the future. Lou was about to say something when she noticed the man.

He was standing some distance away leaning against the back of a stall. He had his back to the fair and was facing them, staring at them in fact. Afterwards, Lou had tried hard to remember what he looked like but all she could picture was his long coat, falling down past his knees. Lou looked behind her for a moment to see what he was staring at.

"I had my first date with a boy when I was thirteen, Lou," Anna said, taking a cigarette out of a packet and putting it in between her lips.

"Oh Mum!" Lou said, embarrassed. Anna was always talking to her about dates and boys.

"His name was Kevin and he always brought his little sister with him, Shirley." Anna lit the cigarette and inhaled.

Lou looked again to where the man had been standing but he had gone. She turned back and finished off her mum's story for her: "And you had to give Shirley a Mars bar every time you wanted to kiss and Shirley grew up overweight and always blamed it on you and Kevin."

"All right, all right," Anna said, scooping the forks and the salt sachets into her pocket. She stood up, the cigarette held between her lips, and brushed down her legs.

"Let's go and do something," she said in a bored voice. "Come on."

It was ten shots for a pound. At the back of the stall was a line of ducks and birds as well as a couple of tiger and lion heads. Lou held her rifle high, closing one eye and aiming for the middle duck. The viewer on the gun was pointing right at its centre and she squeezed the trigger, sure of a bull's-eye.

It missed. The duck cantered off to the right and the stall owner, a man with a patch over one eye, whistled innocently, his hands in the air as if to prove that he had nothing to do with the miss. Lou turned to remonstrate with her mum but her attention was taken by the presence of the man in the long coat again, standing, just a couple of metres away, staring at them, his hands in his pockets. Anna looked round as well but at that moment the man turned his back and walked off into the crowd.

"What's the matter? Who are you looking at?" Anna said, grabbing the rifle and taking her aim.

Lou didn't say but couldn't help scanning the crowd while Anna aimed and shot, aimed and shot, aimed and shot, missing every time.

"This is a con!" she said laughing, handing the man with the patch his rifle back.

"Listen, doll. It's nothing to do with me. Have you ever thought of glasses?"

They walked off, Anna laughing. They headed along the back of the side-shows, along the edge of the fair. After a couple of minutes of dawdling, taking in the fresh, cold air, looking at the distant lights of the streets and houses across the dark common, Lou saw the man again. He was about twenty metres away, leaning against a caravan, his hand languidly stroking a dog. His face was half in shadow, though, and it gave him a look of menace.

Anna saw him too.

Lou felt her stiffen, all the laughter and fun draining out of her. It couldn't have been more than five seconds that they stood facing him, still as statues. That was when Anna grabbed Lou's hand and turned back into the crowd. "Quick!" she hissed, and Lou felt her arm being roughly pulled along.

"Come on!" Anna raised her voice as they dived back into the crowd, passing by groups of young people, old couples, the mums and their toddlers, tired by then, rubbing furiously at their eyes with the backs of their hands.

Lou looked back as they were half walking, half running but all she could see was heads and faces, the man with the long raincoat no longer in sight. Just the revellers, tipping up cans of lager, their laughter exploding from their mouths, flicking the ends of cigarettes into the night, like tiny sparklers in the dark.

"Here!" Anna said, pulling Lou down the alley beside the ghost train, flattening herself against the wooden exterior of the ride.

"Who is he?" Lou said, but Anna didn't answer. She was still holding tightly on to Lou's hand and peering around the corner.

"Mum, who is he?"

"Ssh!" Anna said, needlessly. As if he would hear them above the thundering noise of the rides. She felt Anna's hand tighten on her arm and tensed as they started to walk backwards further away from the crowds. Lou touched Anna's other arm with her free hand and it was like iron, tensed, rigid, her fist clenched as if she were ready to hit out at someone.

Lou put her lips to Anna's ear, "Who is he?" she said, a finger of fear working slowly away at her stomach.

"Just some man from work," Anna said from between clenched lips.

It didn't answer anything, not really. They could hear the cars from the ghost train stagger round the tracks inside and occasionally the fake howls of terror from the people, pretending to be scared, squealing just for show.

Then he was standing at the top of the alley, his back to them, his long coat like a mysterious cloak. He was looking around. It would only be a matter of seconds before he turned and there they would be.

Anna whispered, "Follow me, just keep running, as fast as you can," and she took a few steps up the alley towards him, Lou following her. When she got close she put her two arms out in front of her and began to run. Lou looked on in fright as her mum charged into the back of the man and knocked him flying. On the ghost train someone was howling, long and loud, hoots of laughter in the background.

And they ran, through the people, round by the

dodgems, past the hot dog and fish and chip stands. They ran, round by the hoopla and the mini baseball, the darts and the giant teddy raffle.

Out of the fair they sped across the grass, leaving the bright lights behind them and disappearing into the darkness, no longer holding hands, just tearing through the night towards the street lamps of the town, the buses and the cars, the shops and the houses.

When they got to the street, Anna pulled Lou along the road and into a side alley. In the dark they both stood, looking towards the common, mostly dark but with the lights from the fair in a cluster in the distance.

They stood like that for a few minutes. Lou knew what Anna was waiting for. She too stood rigid against the wall and looked hard into the darkness. A couple of times she thought she saw him emerging, his cloak swirling in the black mists, his face ghastly white and his lips blood red.

He didn't come, though.

After a few minutes Anna leant against a wall and got a cigarette out. "It's nothing to worry about. It's just some bloke from work. Nothing for you to be concerned about."

But all the way home Anna was quiet and when they got into the flat she double-locked the front door and tipped one of the chairs up against it.

That night they slept together, Anna and Lou, curled up together under the duvet.

TWO

When Lou was fifteen she and her mum moved to London. She had to leave a lot of things behind. The peach satin bra and knicker set sat in the middle of a pile of jumble. It didn't fit any more. It had been washed so often that it had lost all its colour. Lou had new things that had replaced it. She folded it carefully, though, running her finger along the soft fabric, feeling a moment's indecision before she pushed it down inside a grey plastic bag. It was hard to discard things but it had to be done. Anna had said so.

It was the seventh time they had moved. At least, that was as far back as Lou could remember. A succession of flats in high rise blocks and then one on top of a menswear shop. The last one, a tiny council house with a garden on the edge of an estate.

The new flat in London was in the basement of a huge Victorian house.

Lou staggered into the new living room with a giant cardboard box that felt as if it was full of bricks. On the outside, in felt tip, were the words *linen and towels*. They had never been so organized. Anna was outside taking stuff from the back of the small van that she had hired. Most of it was on the pavement waiting for Lou to carry it in. A fragile wicker chair sat beside an aluminium pot stand, beside that a giant palm plant that they would have to struggle in with together.

"What about some tea?" Anna said later, holding the kettle up, like some treasure she had found.

Lou was pleased to stop all the carrying, to relax, to look around the huge rooms that she and Anna were going to live in. She looked at the stuff that was strewn about the living-room floor, mostly boxes and suitcases filled with clothes and books and dishes. Even though it was all carefully packed she couldn't help being reminded of all the other times she had bundled their belongings up; into black plastic bags, holdalls, carrier bags. She and her mum stealing away from a flat in the middle of the night or achingly early in the morning; creeping away to avoid paying rent or bills. Pulling the front door to for the last time, crouching down to slide the key under the mat.

Then it was a walk and a train ride or, once, a long coach trip to the next address.

"Gypsies we are!" her mum often said. "Real travellers!"

Part of the journey between addresses was always tense. Anna talking rapidly but her eyes seeming to look past Lou, over her shoulder, behind her at passers-by. She smoked a lot then, too, one long cigarette after another, averting her head from Lou so that she could blow the smoke off into the other direction.

As they got closer to their new address she seemed to soften and talked about the future. "This new place, Lou, this'll be good for us," she had said, on some previous trip.

Lou had nodded, her arm linked tightly through Anna's, her head against her warm shoulder.

"This time we'll put down roots and I'll make some money. We'll be able to buy our own place soon."

Lou had mumbled something in reply. It might happen; it could happen.

Anna really seemed like two different people. Sometimes she was carefree and childlike, more like a friend than a mother. At other times, always when they were travelling to some new place, she was irritable and tense, her lips pursed into a straight worry line. Lou found her own mood affected by the journey, weaving her fingers in and out of each other, cracking her knuckles, banging her nails against her teeth, the train or bus speeding towards some strange place, some new future.

The moves had left Lou with a succession of lost friends, promises to write, to visit when they'd settled again. There'd never been any contact though, no letters written, no stamps bought, no walking to the postbox or waiting for the postman to drop the replies through her front door.

She'd seen the inside of six schools, the buildings different but the wall displays startlingly similar in each one: autumn leaves and conkers with pieces of brown and gold silk draped across; cotton wool for snow and red felt for Father Christmas's coat; the glittering dragons for Chinese New Year.

When she was older the secondary schools had the same bare walls splashed with graffiti, the same loud boys strutting the corridors, the same teachers who rushed away for their coffee and called her Lucy or Liz.

This time, though, they were going to settle.

"The job is as a warden in a women's hostel. There's a flat that goes with it, not on the premises but round the corner, in a big old house. It's brilliant. It'll save us a lot of money. We can buy our own place in a couple of years!" Anna had said, showing Lou the letter. She'd taken a strand of her hair from the side of her head and had wound it round her finger.

The flat was in the basement. There were stairs that led down from the street. Lou had found herself running up and down them several times, admiring the heavy front door, looking hard at the number, making sure it was right.

When the van was finally emptied, Anna came in and picked up her mug of tea.

"I've decided," she said, "to give up smoking. It's a disgusting habit."

In her hand there was an unopened packet of cigarettes, still wrapped in cellophane. She threw it on to the mantelpiece.

"It stays there," she said. "Unopened."

"Why not throw it away," Lou said, "in case you're tempted?"

"That's not really giving up, Lou. That's just depriving yourself. This way, if they stay there, unopened, for a week, a month, a year, then it will really be a victory."

They unpacked their stuff into drawers and cupboards.

Over the years they'd accumulated things: a TV and video, a microwave, a dozen huge cushions that were covered in brightly coloured oriental designs. There were vases and mirrors, pot plants and lamps.

From time to time, while organizing the furniture, Lou saw Anna look furtively at the packet of cigarettes, lying slantwise on the mantelpiece.

"I'll tell you what," she said, finally. "I'll just put this vase here and stand the ciggies behind it. That way they're not that visible. But they're still there and that's what counts."

Counts for what? Lou wanted to ask, but she knew it was some kind of personal contest that Anna was running with herself.

Later, when they'd made the beds up and eaten, they sat on the living-room floor among the cushions.

"I know," Anna said brightly, with just the flicker of a look at the mantelpiece, "let's play our game."

"OK," Lou said, hugging a giant cushion to her chest.

It was a game they'd played for as long as she could remember. Imagine you could buy any ten things that you wanted, which ones would you choose? Sometimes it was toys or records or books; they'd also done cars, holidays and places to live. They both made a mental list and then one by one said what they'd buy.

It gave Lou immense pleasure. There was no cash limit and it meant that for a short while she felt elated, as though she actually owned these things. Anna got excited as the game went on, twisting her hair into a ringlet with her finger.

"I'd buy some jeans. . ."

"A suede coat. . ."

"Silk shirts. . ."

"Boots. . ."

Lou looked around the living room, luxurious in comparison with where they'd lived before. The wallpaper matched the curtains and the kitchen was fitted.

"Leggings. . ."

"Trench coat. . ."

"Skirts. . ."

Maybe this time we *will* settle, she thought, watching her mum pulling clothes from her mental list, using her fingers to count them off.

She lay back against the cushions and felt a fluttering of anticipation in her chest.

This time we will settle.

THREE

Had there been an exact day when Lou had started to distrust Anna? To question the things she said?

The day at Brighton? Or the days that came after?

A trip to the seaside, Anna had said. *Somewhere you've never been before*.

It had been a lie, though. One of many that Lou found out about.

"Lou, have you got the towels? And the sun lotion? Not that we'll need it. The train's going at nine-forty from Victoria. Ruth and Tommy will be round soon. We'll have a picnic lunch."

Lou didn't answer. She was trying, for the third time, to fit the things Anna wanted to take into the shoulder bag. She was thinking quietly to herself about Ruth and her son, Tommy. They had suddenly appeared like fugitives a couple of weeks after Lou and Anna had moved into the flat. They'd followed Anna into the kitchen, large nylon zip-up bags over their shoulders. They were staying the night, Anna had said, before they went to the hostel.

Lou had made them a cup of tea and talked to the little boy.

They'd sat in the corner in their jackets most of the evening, the child eventually falling into a light sleep on his mother's arm. The mother, Ruth, looked nervously around the room as though she expected something to jump out of one of the dark corners.

The next morning they'd gone and Lou had thought no more about it. A few days later, though, Ruth had turned up with a cake she had baked: a Victoria sponge that they'd eaten from some china plates. And now she and Tommy were coming to Brighton with them.

Lou looked over at Anna combing her hair. She was standing in front of the mirror over the mantelpiece, dotting gel on each of her fingertips and pushing them back into her hair to make it stand up. She was also mouthing the words of a song to herself, shaking her head to some imaginary music.

The cigarette packet was still there unopened, several layers of dust on the cellophane around it.

Brighton was chilly. The sun lotion had stayed at the bottom of the bag all day and the four of them had bowed their heads into a wind that had hung on from winter and ambushed them as they turned the corner and headed for the pier.

Ruth and Anna were walking ahead. Tommy was linking Lou's arm and looking up at her with undisguised admiration. He was five and wore small round glasses that constantly needed cleaning. He had an old pillowcase – his "comfort blanket" that he had held under his jacket the whole train journey down to Brighton. He was a nervous little boy and kept asking hypothetical questions like *What would happen if the train didn't stop at the station?* or *What would happen if we were in a boat and there was a storm at sea?*

Ruth didn't seem to notice, though, and just talked on and on to Anna. Lou had tried to catch Anna's eye to see if she was tiring of Ruth's company but she hadn't managed it. After a while of walking along the pier they came to a doughnut stand and bought a bag.

"I love these," Anna said, picking up one of the hot sugary brown rings with the tips of her fingers.

"Me, too," Ruth said. "I'm really glad we came here."

Ruth was tiny, much shorter than Anna. She had a mass of black hair that she tied back with a piece of beaded cord. Bits of it escaped from the front, though, and flew around her head like troublesome insects.

"It's all down to Lou. I told her I'd take her for a treat. Somewhere that she'd never been."

Ruth gave a small chuckle for no apparent reason and continued to eat. Lou looked at the little boy. Tommy was eating his doughnut, his lips covered in sugar, and seemed distracted, as though something was puzzling him. Lou reached over and lifted the tiny glasses off his nose and proceeded to clean them with the end of her T-shirt. Then she used her tissue to wipe the sugar from his face. Tommy linked her arm again and said, "Lou, what would happen if the sea suddenly jumped up over the pier?"

The wind dropped as they turned away from the sea front and into the labyrinth of tiny Lanes that snaked through the town. It was when they were dawdling in front of the antique and jewellery shops that Lou became aware of a feeling of familiarity about the place. It settled on her slowly. The cobblestones on the ground, the dimpled windows in the shops, the signs that hung from the buildings, like festive flags. She began to think that she'd been there before, walked in that very place some other time. The tiny thin streets twisted and turned in front of her and she watched as Tommy ran on, ducking round corners, waiting for them all to catch up.

She saw him up ahead peeking out from behind a shop doorway and in the very back of her mind was reminded of an even smaller child, skipping gaily along the narrow Lanes, wearing a sailor dress that was too long for her.

"Look at this!" Ruth said, from a few metres away.

Lou walked over and in the window of a shop was a giant wooden rocking horse.

"It's old," Anna said.

"Maybe antique," Ruth said. "Must cost a fortune."

"Can I have a ride on it?" Tommy's voice dropped away at the end as though he knew what the answer was going to be. Lou watched him follow after Anna and Ruth and she turned back to the shop and looked at the horse.

It was old, its upholstery worn in places, the tufts of hair so thin you could see through them. Its eyes looked like two dark brown glass marbles, sad and mysterious.

"Ride the horsey, ride the horsey."

Lou heard the voice in the back of her head and looked around as though someone might be there. The others were up at the end of the Lane. Anna waved at her and pointed to the shop they were standing near and then disappeared into it.

She looked back at the horse again and heard the voice, much more insistent this time: *"Ride the horsey!"*

The little girl's dress was navy blue, Lou thought, with a white bib collar and two red ties hanging down from the neck. It was long, well past her knees and too big in places, as though it had really been for someone else, not the little girl at all.

Was *she* the little girl? Lou strained to pull the picture out of her head, closing her eyes for a moment, searching into the darkness for the rest of the memory. Was it her, as a small child, feeling uncomfortable in a new dress that she just had to keep clean, that had prevented her from making sandcastles or collecting shells? The words came again: *"Want to ride the horsey!"*

She looked around, mildly embarrassed at the scenes going on inside her head. As if someone might see her looking stupid, maybe talking to herself, in the middle of Brighton. She was about to walk on, leave the horse to itself, when the woman's voice came gently into her head.

"There, Lou, love. You can't ride the horsey. What would Master Simon say?"

The antique rocking horse seemed to glance out of its left eye at Lou and she stepped back for a moment away from the window. She ignored the wooden toy and focused on her own reflection for a moment. What was she doing hanging around here? Someone would see her and think she was an idiot.

Her own features were only there for a few seconds before the little girl's face took her place. She was angry about not being able to ride on the horse. She'd done it once or twice before, Lou was sure, but this time it wasn't allowed. Master Simon would be upset. Lou watched as the girl's face dropped and she lifted her thumb into the air, looked at it for a second, then popped it into her mouth.

The little girl in the sailor dress disappeared from the glass reflection and Lou knew that she had walked off, in a huff.

Lou wasn't sure, couldn't picture it any more, but the woman had followed the child and was speaking. "*There, my Lou, Lou. We'll come another day, when Master Simon's not so busy.*"

The woman was big, wearing a dress with bright flowers on it, made with several metres of fabric. Lou could hear the rustle of the material as she walked along.

Lou opened her eyes and stood back, away from the shop, the images fading in her head. Then Anna was beside her.

"You coming, Lou? We ought to make tracks to the station."

"Yes," Lou said, watching as Ruth and Tommy came towards her. The four of them walked away, towards Queens Road that would lead up to the station. After a few seconds Lou looked back, half expecting to see her there, the little girl with the sailor dress.

She didn't, though. What caught her eye was the name

of the shop. In big italics, it sloped across the top, *Master Simon's Antiques*.

"*We'll come another day, when Master Simon's not so busy*."

She heard the words in her head and the swish of the dress that the lady was wearing. The lady who'd been looking after her, had taken her out for the day.

"Mum," she said, when there was a quiet moment, when Ruth and Tommy were ahead of them, "are you sure I've never been to Brighton before?"

"Positive!" Anna said, slipping her arm through Lou's. "Here, have a bit of fudge." Anna took out a tissue and unwrapped three bits of fudge, all different types.

"Mum, you didn't take those!" Lou said, shocked.

"No! They were testers, in the shop. They offered them to us so I took a couple of extra bits for you!"

Lou took a piece and put it gingerly in her mouth. Free samples in a fudge shop. It didn't sound likely.

In the train, on the way home, Lou thought about the antique rocking horse and the lady in the flowered dress. Anna was wrong; she must have been there before. When she was a very young child she'd been taken there by someone she knew well.

Why hadn't Anna told her?

Could it be that she'd been with an aunt or someone from her father's family? Was that the woman she had remembered, big and soft with whispering words, her dress made of so many metres of fabric that when she stood close to her leg she could hide in its folds?

Her father's family. What about his mum, his dad,

24

brothers or sisters? There had been some relatives, Lou was sure. Over the years they had been mentioned, only briefly, their names dropped accidentally into the conversation. A moment later, before she had even realized what had been said, Anna had brushed the information aside, tidied it away, packed it up somewhere.

As the train rocked her from side to side she looked across the aisle at Anna, who was saying something into Ruth's ear. It wasn't the sort of thing Anna liked to talk about, *the past*. It was a subject that was guaranteed to cause an upset.

There were no baby photos of Lou, no wedding photos of her parents, no mementoes of her days as a toddler, toys or books.

"When your dad died I had to get rid of it all," Anna had said. "Everything was too painful. That's why we moved. That's why we started afresh."

That's why they left the past behind them. They closed it up like an empty house and walked or ran as quickly and as far away as they could.

The only thing they had was a photo of a man in a uniform who was dead. Lou's father, the soldier.

She felt a nudge at her elbow. Tommy looked up at her, and smiled. Lou reached over and took the tiny plastic glasses and began to clean them.

FOUR

The man in the photograph. Lou often sat and thought about him.

Sergeant Robert Lewis of the Sussex Regiment. He had been in the army for four years when they'd sent him to Northern Ireland. For ten days he'd walked the streets of Belfast before a bomb had blown him apart.

There'd been nothing left of him, Anna had said. They'd just buried the bits and a uniform with a Union Jack over the top.

Lou had been two years old and they had moved away from the army house they'd lived in and started a new life in a different part of the country. It was for the best, Anna had said. She didn't want any memories.

So Lou knew almost nothing about her father, his family, his friends, the place that they had lived. The information, the hard facts that she had, could have fitted on to the back of an envelope.

It bothered her, having no sense of her father. Lots of other girls she had known had lived with their mothers, their fathers living at some other address and visiting at weekends, taking them out to the cinema and McDonald's. But Lou had never known her father, her *dad*. And Anna never wanted to talk about him, only mentioning him accidentally, brushing aside her questions about him.

When other kids in school had talked about their families Lou had slowly joined in, nervously at first, talking about Robert Lewis, her dad. The longer she was at a school the more fluent she became about him. Anna had hidden him away and it had been up to her to make a real person out of him, using only the tiny fragments of information that she had been given.

"My dad's a war hero. . ."

"My dad was a sergeant in the army. . ."

"My dad was very tall, the tallest in the regiment. . ."

"My dad told all the other soldiers to stand back when he heard about the bomb. He went forward slowly, saving their lives by risking his own."

"My dad had lots of money and was going to take me to Disneyland. . ."

Disneyland. It was something other girls often talked about. In Florida it was, or Los Angeles, or Paris. Lou was sure, positive even, that her father would have taken her there if he'd been alive.

Lou had made friends during conversations like these. Other girls who sat with her at lunchtime and whispered gossip and plans. Mary and Kelly; Michelle and Suzy. They had linked arms, stood in corners together, hummed songs, gone shopping, watched TV. They had become friends for months and years. Or so it had seemed to Lou.

But then there was The Move. The new school and the strange girls. The pain Lou felt at losing a friend. The growing rage she felt when Anna didn't allow her to write.

"We can't afford to let anyone know where we've gone, love. I owed money on the rent."

"We don't want the Council Tax people to find out where we are!"

"I had a row with a couple of women at work! I don't want them to find me."

During The Move there was always anger in Lou; like a tiny caged bird it flew about inside her chest. The journey to a new home, hundreds of miles away sometimes, exhausted it and it was replaced by a growing apprehension. The thundering noise of the train, the screeching of brakes from the coach, Anna's thin fingers holding cigarette after cigarette made Lou fearful; the world seemed to be a scary place, full of debt collectors and strange places where they had to go and live, to start all over again.

Then it was just Anna and Lou again. The friends and people they knew were left behind in another place that they would never return to. Her father, his memory, was shut away then, like his photograph, packed up in Lou's suitcase, in between her old school clothes.

Anna and Lou, like two sisters, not mother and daughter: like best friends.

And Anna, even though she wouldn't talk about Lou's father, had never replaced him, not really. There had been no new stepfather. Their bathroom cabinet had only ever been full of women's things: deodorant, talc, a small lady shave, packets of tampons, Body Shop soaps scattered like rhinestone jewels along the shelves. There had been no shaving foam or aftershave, no man's razor or beard trimmer, none of the chunky combs or brushes that she had seen in other bathrooms.

One or two men had stayed occasionally, the most recent one when they'd been living over the menswear shop. His name was Dougie and Lou had got used to seeing his jackets hanging round the backs of chairs and his shirts hanging over the radiators. It was a time when her mother's door was often locked and when she did go in she saw his giant shoes peeping out from beneath the big bed.

"We're all right on our own, aren't we?" Anna had whispered, after he'd stopped coming around.

Lou had nodded, even though sometimes it seemed lonely just the two of them. She found herself getting her father's photo out of the bottom drawer and studying it closely. She imagined his voice, deep and powerful. He had laughed a lot, she was sure. He'd probably played with her when she'd been very small, had carried her high up on his shoulders, holding on to a leg with each hand. Sometimes she imagined another photo, the three of them in Disneyland, her dad holding her hand, his other arm around Anna's shoulder, just like a real family.

When she'd been much younger his photo had sat in its frame in the living room of whatever place they'd lived in. Over the years, though, it had been moved out of the way, had collected dust on a shelf in one of her bedrooms.

Before the last move, Lou had noticed how old and tatty the frame was looking and had suggested to Anna that they buy a new one. She'd even said that she would pay for it.

"No, don't be silly. It's perfectly all right!" Anna had said in an offhand manner.

A lump had formed in Lou's throat and she had kept her mouth tightly shut in case something nasty should fly out; sharp words were forming, lining up. *WHY CAN'T I HAVE A NEW FRAME FOR MY DAD'S PHOTOGRAPH?* she'd wanted to shout. But Anna had given her a hug and then, breathing hard on the glass of the frame, took a tissue and gave it a little polish.

"There," she'd said. "Good as new!"

Lou had forgiven her immediately. The anger had disappeared like a puff of smoke. Because, more than anyone in the world, Lou loved Anna. She'd have been embarrassed to say it, wouldn't have admitted it to her closest schoolfriend, but it was true. Sometimes the feeling weighed her down like a great burden. Other times it filled her up until she thought it would burst out of her.

After the last move the frame had stayed in a suitcase and then had been unpacked into a drawer. On the Saturday after Brighton, when Lou had finished her breakfast, she made a decision to get it out and place it on the mantelpiece, near the untouched cigarettes.

She polished it with a damp cloth and stood back a few times to see what angle it should sit at. Finally, when she was pleased with it, she sat down and looked at it.

Sergeant Robert Lewis. Her father who had died being a hero.

*

Later Anna came in wearing her dressing gown.

"Lou, love, will you do me a favour?" In her hand there were some keys. "Would you go over to Ruth's old flat? Tommy needs more of his clothes and Ruth doesn't feel up to going there. The caretaker, Bob, will go in with you. Just pop in and pick up the stuff in the two top drawers in the small bedroom. You could also pick up the letters and see if she's got any phone messages."

Lou took the keys. "What if her husband's around?" she said.

"I doubt very much that he will be. It's been weeks since she left. Anyway, there's a court order preventing him going near her home. Bob will be there. He's a nice man. He knows about Ruth's situation."

"OK," Lou said, noticing Anna's gaze fixing on the photo of her dad that she'd put on the mantelpiece.

"Why on earth have you got that old thing out?" Anna said.

"I thought it would be nice," Lou said steadily.

Anna looked at the photo without expression. "You silly, sentimental thing," she said finally, and put her arm around Lou's shoulder. She had a sleepy smell and her hair was tousled. Lou breathed a sigh of relief. The photo hadn't caused any upset. She picked up Ruth's keys from the table and went upstairs.

Ruth's old flat was a short bus ride away. Lou had been there once with her mum a couple of weeks before, when Ruth and Tommy had first moved into the hostel. They'd been careful going in and coming out, afraid that Ruth's ex-husband might be around and come after Ruth. Some violent men went to great lengths, her mum said.

Bob, the caretaker, stood beside Lou as she opened Ruth's front door and picked up the mail from the mat. He was a tall, thin man with wiry grey hair and a wrinkled T-shirt that said Southend United. He was yawning a lot, stretching his arms up into the air until Lou could hear his bones clicking. It was clear that he'd just pulled himself out of bed.

"I'll wait here," he said, smoothing his T-shirt down with his hand.

Lou went straight into the small bedroom. She emptied the drawers of Tommy's underwear and T-shirts. From the shelf she picked a small stuffed monkey and some model cars. She filled up a couple of canvas bags and was about to let herself out when she remembered the phone messages. She put the bags down by the front door and saw that Bob was sitting on the nearby stairs, his head leaning against the banisters.

She walked back towards the hall telephone. The tiny green light was blinking on and off on the answerphone. She found a pen and got ready to write notes on the back of an envelope.

There was only one message. It was a man's voice, dark and hard as metal.

"Ruth, there's no point in hiding. I'll find you in the end."

That was all. No hello or goodbye.

Lou played it over three times. Each time the voice

sounded angrier, meaner. The pen was limp in her hands. She didn't write it down. She chucked the envelope away and walked out of the flat.

"You all right?" Bob said, getting up off the step. "You got everything you wanted?"

Lou nodded and walked ahead of him out of the building. She heard the heavy street door click behind her and felt a ball of uneasiness lodge in her chest. The court order hadn't stopped Ruth's husband reaching out for her through the phone lines. She found herself looking over her shoulder as she walked away from the house, her steps hurrying towards the bus stop. For a brief moment she was reminded of the funfair that they had gone to two years before, the man from Anna's work that they had run away from; taking steps and looking back, hiding round corners and peeking out, making a run across the grass, not looking round, just hoping that he wasn't there.

A couple of days later they'd left the area. Anna hadn't wanted to go back to work and face the man.

As she waited for the bus she thought about Ruth's husband. His voice on the answerphone was calm and cold. They had been divorced for three years, Anna had said, and yet he still came around to cause trouble. He had broken Ruth's door down and hit her. He had even threatened Tommy once. The police had told him to stay away but he had ignored them. He'd followed Ruth to work and back and had said he'd take Tommy to another country. "Make sure you don't say any of this to little Tommy," Anna had said.

Lou felt the beginnings of a shiver and remembered his words, *I'll find you in the end.*

Those words would upset Ruth, Lou was sure. They had only to touch on the subject of her ex-husband and Ruth began to chew at her thumb, and fidget with her hair. She'd get up and walk to the window, looking casually out, but Lou knew that she was checking that her husband wasn't there, that he hadn't found her.

When she got home, Arthur, the maintenance man from the hostel, was moving a filing cabinet into the flat. He was very old, sixty or more, but Lou liked him because he was friendly and funny. He was being helped by a young man whom Lou hadn't seen before. The tin cabinet was blocking the tiny hallway. Lou could see Anna clearing a place for it in the living room.

"Come past, Lou," she shouted. "Ruth, Lou's here with Tommy's things."

The two men moved aside to let Lou past. Arthur looked like someone's grandad. He had a pencil behind one ear and a tiny butt of a cigarette sticking out of one corner of his mouth. The other man was much younger, his hair pulled back into a ponytail, the earphones of a Walkman hung carelessly around his neck.

"Have you met my nephew, Lulu?" Arthur said. "One of them students. Charlie's his name."

"Hi!" Lou said, squeezing along the hall.

"Sure you can manage those bags?" the young man said to Lou, smiling broadly at her. He had dozens of teeth.

"Course I can!" she said, looking awkwardly at him.

"Everything all right?" Anna appeared. "You can carry it through now, Arthur, I've made a space."

"Right you are, Annie," Arthur said.

Anna rolled her eyes at Lou. "I've told him it's Anna," she said, shaking her head. "How did you get on at Ruth's? Any problems?"

"No," Lou said, standing aside so that the men could carry the cabinet past her. She placed the two bags on the floor.

"Any phone messages?"

Ruth had come out of the kitchen and was standing in the doorway, an apron on and a large chopping knife in her hand. She was looking past them and eyeing the two men warily, as though she suspected one of them of being her husband in disguise.

"No, none," Lou said.

It wasn't the right time to tell her.

FIVE

The day Lou found the letter and the photograph. That had been a few weeks after the visit to Brighton with Ruth and Tommy.

A little girl, two years old, maybe a bit more, sitting on the knee of a woman. A navy blue sailor dress with a white bib and red ties at the front. The woman's face round and cheerful, her hair short and curly.

The woman's dress full and flowery, her arm, dimpled, fat even. The little girl, fair-haired, pretty; a thumb in her mouth, her lips puckered around it.

Without thinking Lou had slotted her own thumb into her mouth. She hadn't done it for a long time but it felt comfortable. She sat like that for some time, thinking.

Even though they'd been moved for over a month there were still a couple of boxes to unpack. Before Lou started sorting through the stuff she took another look at the letter that had come that morning from the local comprehensive school.

"*I am pleased to inform you that a place is available for your daughter, Louise Lewis, to join this school. She should start on Monday, June 26th at 9 a.m. She should arrive at the main school office where she will be introduced to her new form tutor. . .*"

Lou let the letter drop out of her hand and sighed.

Anna had been adamant that she should return to school before September. They'd just had a row about it before she left.

"You can't sit around here for months not doing anything," she'd said, sorting through her files and bits of paper.

"I wouldn't be doing nothing. I could read, go to the library. I could look after the flat, shop, cook."

"Apart from anything else it's illegal. You are supposed to go to school!" Anna's voice was starting to get an edge to it. She was picking up books and files from the table and putting them down again. She was looking for something.

"But there's only a few weeks to the end of term," Lou said, following her into the kitchen and then back into the living room. "Then it'll be the summer holidays. What's the point of me starting so near the end of the year? It's embarrassing, starting in the middle of everything. I could start in September. Then I wouldn't feel so bad."

"And then in September," Anna said, picking up a piece of paper and fitting it into a file, "in September, there'll be another reason why you don't want to go. I've had this for years, Lou. You've got a whole sack full of reasons why you shouldn't go to school."

"No, I haven't," Lou said, defensively. Anna snapped her case shut and stood looking at her.

"I want you to go to school. Your education is important."

"I don't want to start a few weeks from the end of the year!"

"But you're studying for exams next year! It's vital that you're there!"

"If it's so vital," Lou said, hardly knowing whether she had the courage to get the next words out, "how come you've spent years dragging me out of schools? As soon as I'm settled, as soon as I'm doing well, as soon as I've made friends, then we have to leave!"

Anna's expression faltered for a moment and she let her case drop on to its side and sat down on the chair. She put two fingers up to her lips, as though she was holding an invisible cigarette. She seemed to be thinking, on the verge of saying something, but no words came out. Eventually, after a long silence, her eyes seemed to glass over and she said, "You don't know everything, Lou. I've done my best for you, for us."

Lou felt a sting of remorse. Seeing Anna cry always made her feel light-headed, faint.

"I'm sorry," she said, her voice business-like. "I'll go to school. I'll go next Monday." She knelt down on the floor beside Anna's knees. "I really am sorry."

Anna nodded her head but her lips were pursed into a tiny rosebud. She didn't look convinced.

"I'll go next Monday, I promise," Lou said, standing up. She took Anna's hands and pulled her back to her feet. "You get off to work, you'll be late."

It wasn't worth rowing about.

Lou found the photograph and letter in a handbag that she'd pulled out of the bottom of a very old cardboard box. It was part of the stuff that had been stored at a friend of Anna's for a number of years. It was thick with dust and on the side were the words THIS WAY UP in felt tip. At the top of the box were a number of pieces of china: a cup and saucer, a small jug, a plate, a couple of side plates, all wrapped in sheets of newspaper. There was also a thin crystal vase. Lou took the fragile objects carefully over to the sink and washed them individually, leaving them upside down to dry.

The discarded newspapers were all over the living-room floor and she swept them up in her hands. She was about to throw them away when she glanced at the date on the top of one of the yellowing pages.

The newspapers were more than twelve years old. She laid them on the floor and straightened one or two of them out. There were photographs of current prominent people, usually politicians, who looked much younger, thinner with no grey hair. She recognized articles on TV soaps and the names of characters she knew.

On the back page there was an article about "The Troubles". The second headline said WHAT FUTURE FOR NORTHERN IRELAND?

The box must have been packed up twelve years before and never opened. She spread the newspaper pages out flat on the floor, scanning them for any item on a dead soldier, killed in Northern Ireland. There was nothing, though. They were mostly pages from tabloids; one even had a picture of a half-naked woman on it. A couple of sheets were from a local paper: THE WEEKLY ADVERTISER. Shoreham edition.

Anna had used this paper to wrap things up when she'd left the army house after Lou's dad had been killed. Did that mean that the house was in Shoreham? Wherever that was?

She found the letter and photograph in the zip compartment of the black handbag. The photograph was slightly blurred but Lou could see the face of the woman; friendly and smiling, her eyes crinkled up in the sunlight.

The child was small with balloon cheeks and her hair had been pulled up into two bunches. Each had a red ribbon which matched the ties on the sailor dress. She had her hands together as though in prayer but the delighted smile on her face suggested that she might have been in the middle of clapping. Lou looked hard at the photo. Was this a photo of her, as a child? The only photo there was?

She got up and went to the bookshelves for an atlas of the British Isles. It only took a few seconds to look up Shoreham in the index and then she saw it on the map in front of her. About an inch away from Brighton. Twenty miles.

The letter didn't help much.

The Tulips,
Swallow Drive,
Shoreham.

Dear Jill,

Just a line to let you know how we're getting on down here on the windswept south coast. The family's well. You should see how big Lou is! You won't recognize her when you see her!

*The most amazing thing is that I'm going to have a baby.
With Lou so young I won't know which way to turn!*

I hope you're looking after yourself.

Much love, Sal.

The woman's name was Sal. Lou said the word over a couple of times, Sal, Sally, but no memories came. The letter was addressed to Jill. Why did her mother have a letter in her bag addressed to someone else?

Dear Jill. . . You should see how big Lou is. . .

Lou took her thumb out of her mouth and put the letter and the photograph in the bottom of her jewellery box. She had no idea what she was going to do with them.

SIX

The hostel was attacked the following Monday morning.

The brick came through the office window, making a loud crashing sound. It bounced on the wooden floor a couple of times before skidding to a stop at the corner of Anna's desk.

Lou was in her school uniform, about to leave for her first day at the comprehensive. She'd called into the office to say goodbye to Anna, who'd been working since before seven that morning.

Lou glanced down at the brick, shaken, startled, but not sure of what had happened. It was dark red, chipped at the edges, leaving a skid mark on the floor.

There was a split second of silence as it came to a halt, the tinkling from the broken glass subsiding. Everything seemed to stand very still.

Then a voice broke through the quiet, shattering the unreal calm. "SANDRA! SANDRA! SANDRA!" it screamed, and Lou felt the words hit against the side of her head like flying debris.

Anna pulled herself up from her desk, her mouth open in a silent gasp.

"Get the police," she said, her lips hardly moving.

She turned round and picked up a large walking stick that sat in the corner behind her. Lou grabbed the receiver from the desk and pressed the buttons: nine, nine, nine. "Police, please. The women's hostel in Collis Street is being attacked," she gasped. Anna was by the window, the walking stick in her hand like a baton. From upstairs Lou could hear the crying of a couple of the kids and still the voice, through the front door, interspersed with banging.

"SANDRA! SANDRA! PLEASE, SANDRA!"

A young woman rushed into the office just as Anna was going out. Her face had a shocked look on it. Over her shoulder she had a tiny child.

"Anna, he's found me! Anna. . ."

"It's all right, Sandra. The police are on their way."

Lou put the receiver down. The young woman was looking frantically round the office. Lou didn't know what to say so she walked across to her and held her arm gingerly round the woman's shoulder but Ruth came in then and said, "Sandra, quick! Out the back. We'll keep him at the door."

"SANDRA! SANDRA! BLOODY WELL SPEAK TO ME!"

Sandra scuttled out of the door, followed by Anna and Lou. Some other women came running along the corridor, eyeing the front door fearfully:

"*What's happening?*"

"*Who is it?*"

"*Is it my Ron?*"

"*It's Sandra's boyfriend.*"

"*He'll be through the door in a minute.*"

Lou was out in the hall, behind Anna, who had the walking stick raised in the air. She could see, through the leaded glass, the shape of the man. He looked like a giant.

"SANDRA, I KNOW YOU'RE IN THERE! I'LL BREAK THIS BLOODY DOOR DOWN!"

The women seemed to edge together, Lou stepping back, away from the door. Anna was in front of her, like the leader of a pack of fighters, her arm raised in the air, the walking stick like a sword.

The sirens blasted from just metres away, as if the police cars had crept up silently and only turned the sound on at the last minute. The man's silhouette disappeared from the door and they could hear shouting from outside. Anna flung the front door open and there, just outside the gate, were two policemen holding the man between them.

All the women crowded out, along the pathway. A couple of the small kids were still crying. One of the policemen was talking into his radio. The blue light on the top of the car was turning eerily. It reminded Lou of a carousel ride; she thought, for a second, of the fairground, on a cold spring evening when she and Anna were chased away from the rides by a man in a long dark coat.

The man the police were holding wasn't a giant at all. He was small and thin and was wearing a suit, as though he was on his way to a job in an office. He was mumbling to himself, a low monologue about Sandra which neither of the policemen seemed to be listening to. Lou noticed that his jacket was done up on the wrong button and the collar of his shirt was flicking up.

A WPC had come running along the street and Anna was talking to her, looking back towards the man. The group of women opened up in front of Lou and Sandra went through. She didn't have her baby over her shoulder. She stood looking at the man.

"Sandra," he said softly when he saw her.

"That's enough from you," one of the policemen said and pulled him towards the car. Sandra gripped on to Lou's arm. On the other side was Ruth, who leaned across and ruffled Sandra's hair.

"He's gone now, Sand," she said.

But Sandra had started to cry.

"I'll have to move now, won't I? I'll have to find somewhere else!"

The police-car doors slammed shut and it moved slowly away up the street, its light still pulsing. Anna and the WPC came towards the group of women.

"Let's go in now, shall we?" Anna said calmly, a stiff smile on her face. "We've got some clearing up to do."

Lou felt a hand clasp hers. She looked down and saw Tommy, without his glasses, smiling up at her. "Do you think that man had a gun, Lou?" he said, his eyes wide open.

"No, I don't think so," Lou said, following the group of women back up the path and into the house.

Later that morning Lou took the broken glass out in a box and put it down by the bins. Tommy was following her around. Inside, some of the women and their children were huddled together in the back television lounge. A couple of WPCs were sitting among them talking quietly. One of them had her notepad open and was writing things in it.

In the office, Arthur was measuring up the window for new glass. He was squatting down and had a rolled-up newspaper sticking out of his back pocket. When he saw her, he said, "Some blokes, they want horse whippin'."

Anna was on the phone.

"Inspector, I need some help here, more regular patrols, more presence. Some of the women are very fragile. I can't have them feeling vulnerable." She had a pencil in her hand and was pointing it at the mouth of the receiver. She beckoned to Lou to sit down.

Lou sat down and Tommy leaned against her. She noticed the badge: *ANNA LEWIS PROJECT WORKER*. She didn't usually bother to wear it.

"OK, Inspector. I'd be really grateful."

The phone "tinged" as Anna replaced the receiver.

"Thanks for helping out, Lou. It's been hectic. I'm just so relieved that no one got hurt."

"Should be locked up and the key thrown away," Arthur said, standing up.

"I appreciate you coming so promptly, Arthur."

"That's all right, Annie, no problem. My Charlie'll go and get the glass and we'll have it fixed this afternoon."

'Well, don't worry about Tommy. I'll look after him," Lou said.

Her mum gave her a look of gratitude for a moment. Then, remembering something, she looked at her watch.

"It's ten o'clock! You're late for your first day at school!"

"But this is an emergency," Lou said. "I'll go tomorrow. I promise."

"You will as well," her mum said and was about to continue when the phone rang. She picked it up and immediately adopted a new, crisp voice. "Anna Lewis speaking."

Lou walked out of the office into the hall, holding Tommy's hand. She could see Ruth and Sandra sitting in a small huddle with some other women in the living room. Lou knew that Sandra would disappear now, that Anna would find her a place in another hostel and her boyfriend would start looking for her all over again.

She remembered Ruth's husband's words: *Ruth, there's no point in hiding. I'll find you in the end.*

She pursed her lips. It wasn't a good time to tell them now.

Anna came home late, after taking Ruth and Tommy back to the hostel. She looked tired. Her hair was pulled back in an elastic band and her face was pale.

"The window's been replaced; the women have settled down." She was ticking things off on her fingers.

Lou handed her a steaming mug of tea. She was trying to decide when would be a good time to bring up the issue of school.

"Tomorrow I've got to go to the police station with poor Sandra. She needs to give a statement. Then I'll have to find her another placement. She won't want to stay now that he knows where she is."

"About school. . ." Lou decided to try and slide the subject in.

"Oh!" Anna stopped drinking her tea. "Ruth's starting a course this week and she hasn't yet got Tommy fixed up with a childminder. I said he could stay in the office tomorrow but I need to be with Sandra. Damn!"

"A course?"

"In computers. She's been a secretary for years. She wants to do something better. What am I going to do with Tommy?"

"I could stay in the hostel, look after him," Lou said.

"You'll be at school."

"What I thought was," Lou interrupted quickly, "it would be awful to start in the middle of the week, since I missed today, through no fault of my own. It'll be in the middle of the timetable and it'll be awkward. Why don't I start next Monday? That makes sense. Then I could look after Tommy for the rest of this week. Ruth'll have time to find a real childminder!"

"Tuesday is not exactly the middle of the week," Anna said, but Lou could see by the way she leant back against the chair that it wasn't going to be too much of an argument.

"I'd have to find out where to pay dinner money and stuff and that'll mean I'll be out of lessons. I'll have to walk in late, it'll be embarrassing. You've said yourself, in the past, that it's better to start on Monday."

"Have I?" Anna lifted her head off the back of the chair. It was meant to be a look of annoyance but it was half-hearted.

"So it will be better if I looked after Tommy. I could keep him amused."

"I'm sure you could."

"Then I'll start school next Monday. I promise."

Anna's eyes narrowed and she clicked her tongue against the roof of her mouth.

"Don't think you've put one over on me. You'll be at that school next Monday morning if I have to drag you there myself."

"Absolutely," Lou said, a look of incomprehension on her face, as though she didn't understand Anna's suspicions. Inside her head there was glee, like a tiny cartoon character leaping about with joy.

No school for a week and all she had to do was look after Tommy!

Later, before going to bed, she went into Anna's room and sat under the duvet with her. It was something she hadn't done for a while. When she had been small Anna used to come into her bed and snuggle up, her big legs making a tent in the bedclothes. As she grew bigger it became difficult for them to fit into her single bed, so Lou usually went into her mum's big double one.

"Mum?" she said, not sure whether to bring the subject up or not.

"Um?" Anna was reading something from the newspaper.

"My dad's family. Where did they come from?"

"Why on earth do you ask that? Now of all times."

"I was just thinking about him. About them. Whether he might have had any sisters."

"It was a long time ago," her mum said, which didn't seem to answer any question.

"So, he didn't have anyone who lived, say, in Brighton?"

Anna put the newspaper down and turned to her. She looked puzzled. Just for a second Lou thought she saw a flash of anger.

"Brighton?"

"For argument's sake." Lou's voice was faltering. She moved a bit closer to Anna's warm body.

"No," Anna said, pulling the duvet up around her knees, moving her elbows so that they seemed to dig into Lou's legs.

"I just wondered," Lou said and linked her hand through her arm. She let her head lie back on the pillow.

Anna sat forward, her shoulders and back hunched, her body no longer soft but full of sharp angles. After a few moments like that she lay back on the pillow and Lou fitted her head into her shoulder.

"It's just me and you, Lou. That's what's really important."

Lou said nothing. Her dad wasn't any part of their lives at all. He was just a face in a frame, not a real person who'd lived and breathed. Anna had buried him when Lou was only two years old. She had also buried all the memories of their life together. Anna had decided that Lou was never to find out about her father.

It wasn't right but Lou didn't want to push it, didn't want to upset Anna, to see her cry or feel the sharp edge of her shoulder as she turned away from her.

All she wished was that she knew a bit more about him.

It wasn't much to ask.

SEVEN

The next morning Anna had planned to go to the police station with Sandra. Lou was sitting in the office while she got ready to leave.

"Are you sure you don't mind staying here with Tommy for a few hours? You could answer the phones for me. Some of the women are going to the park later. You could take Tommy, if you like."

Tommy was on the floor in the middle of a pile of Lego. One of the other young boys was sitting with him. There were a number of half-made spaceships scattered around the carpet.

"Arthur's making a start on the attic room. He said that Charlie is coming in later to give him a hand," Anna said, looking at her watch. "After yesterday, it's not really the best time for a strange man to come into the house but . . . as long as Arthur's here. . ."

"OK," Lou said, looking at the phone with its buttons and lights.

"You know how to use the switchboard. Every call should be written down in the book. Write the time it came in as well. I'd better be off. I'll be back in a couple of hours."

"OK," said Lou.

At first, after Anna left, Lou was tense, looking rapidly from Tommy to the phone switchboard and back again. A couple of times she got up and walked across to the big bay window, looking at the new glass and the soft putty around the edges.

Two phone calls came, one after the other, both for women in the hostel. Lou had the list of their code names in the drawer by the phone. Callers could only be put through if they knew the correct code name. Her mum had told her the idea was to protect the women from unwelcome callers.

Lou let her eye scan the list. Ruth's code name was Susan White. If anyone rang and asked for any of the women by their real name she was to say that they had no such person staying there.

It was cloak and dagger stuff and Lou felt a momentary thrill at being part of it. Then she felt a gloom descend when she remembered what her mum had told her about the women in the hostel.

They're all victims, Lou. They've been physically hurt by men who said they loved them. These woman are safe in the hostel. That's why we keep their identities secret.

The next couple of phone calls were for Anna and Lou wrote the messages, in her best handwriting, in the book.

The doorbell rang just as she replaced the receiver on the last call. She went to the window and looked out. Charlie was standing looking at a newspaper.

Lou opened the door. "Hello," she said nervously, looking up at him. "It's Charlie, isn't it?"

"Yep," he said. "Lulu?" He pulled an earphone out of his ear and let it hang over his shoulder.

"Well, not. . ." Lou was about to put him right about her name but she noticed that he'd left the other earphone in and seemed to be preoccupied, moving his head in time with the beat of a song. She stood back while he took a light denim jacket off and hung it on one of the hooks in the hallway. When he turned away from her she could see his hair, pulled tightly back into a ponytail at the nape of his neck.

"Arthur's already here, up in the attic." Lou found herself pulling her own hair back into an imaginary ponytail. Then she let it go and suddenly wasn't sure what to do with her hands.

"Yep," Charlie said. He was half humming the tune, part of which Lou could hear, distantly, from the earphone that was hanging down.

"Mum said you knew where all the paint and stuff was."

"Yep, OK, Lulu," he said and smiled at her, showing lots of teeth. Lou ran her tongue over her own teeth while she looked at him.

"My name's Lou actually," she said. "Not Lulu."

"Lou?" he said, pulling the other earphone out, and looking hard at her.

"Yes. Not that it's important." She felt herself reddening.

"OK, *Lou*. I'll just go up to Arthur."

"Yes, only Mum says to be sensitive, you know, because of the trouble we had here yesterday."

"Absolutely. Sensitive, *Lou*," Charlie said, fiddling with his Walkman.

She watched him walk up the stairs with an odd,

unsettled feeling. Looking round she noticed that his jacket was hanging awkwardly on the hooks. She walked across and straightened it, her fingers lingering on the fabric for a moment.

After a number of phone calls, one from Anna to check that she was all right, Lou made a pot of tea and called Arthur down. Tommy was curled up in an armchair, looking at a book about spiders. The other boy had gone off with his Lego models.

"Here," she said, handing Arthur a steaming mug of tea.

"Thanks, Lulu," he said. Arthur seemed to have a knack for getting people's names wrong. He pulled his newspaper from his back pocket and backed on to a chair to sit down. Just then Charlie came in and Lou picked up the second mug of tea, her hand shaking slightly, and handed it to him.

"Sugar?" she said, glancing up at his face, her eyes darting about, unsure where to rest.

"Nope. I'm sweet enough," he said. He leant against one of the far desks and Lou noticed his long legs splayed out, taking up a lot of space in the room.

Arthur was looking at them over his mug of tea.

"What do you make of this young man, Lulu? Don't you think he's handsome?" Arthur guffawed at this statement and Lou found herself blushing at the attention. Charlie had put his earphones in and was nodding his head in time with a song that she couldn't hear.

"Watch him, Lulu. He's a one for the ladies, he is." Arthur

opened his newspaper and disappeared behind it. All Lou could see was his legs. She flicked her eyes back towards Charlie and caught him looking straight at her. She looked down immediately and shuffled some papers on Anna's desk. She had an uncomfortable feeling, as though there was a spotlight on her and she was about to do something embarrassingly stupid. Then she remembered something.

"Mum said I had to give you some time sheets to fill in. I'll just get them."

She got up and went to the filing cabinet. Behind her she could hear the rustle of the paper and Arthur's voice, "Good girl, Lulu."

The filing cabinet was messy. Some files had been pulled out of alphabetical order and replaced at the front. Lou soon found the file marked TIME SHEETS. She took it out and laid it on the desk.

"Hello there, young Tom. You lost your tongue today?" She heard Arthur's voice.

"He's reading his book," Lou said, and was about to close the filing cabinet drawer when her eye was caught by a file that was tucked in the back. On it were the words, PERSONNEL: Anna Lewis. Confidential.

She paused for a minute and then closed the drawer. She handed the forms to Arthur.

"Right!" he said. Taking the forms he folded them up inside the newspaper which he then used to hit Charlie playfully on the shoulder.

"Back to work, boy!" he said. "That's how you keep your workers under control. Don't you, Tom lad?"

Charlie drank his tea down and smiled good-humouredly, rolling his eyes. Lou found herself smiling back at him, her previous embarrassment gone. Charlie had a lot to put up with. She listened as they walked slowly up the stairs. Arthur was talking but there was no sound from Charlie except heavy footsteps.

Once they were gone Lou turned back to the filing cabinet. She took Anna's file from the drawer and laid it on the desk.

"Lou, what would happen if a tarantula walked across the floor now?" Tommy said. It was the first time he had spoken for ages. Lou looked over at him. He had his book to the side and was looking down on to the floor, his eyes zigzagging back and forth.

"We'd have to capture it, I expect," Lou said, picking the cardboard file up. Inside was a printed application form that had been filled out by Anna. Her mum's name, her age, qualifications, her previous jobs. It was written in neat black pen, in bold, printed letters. ANNA LEWIS applying for the post of PROJECT LEADER, 33-year-old single parent. Lou scanned the page and then turned over. There were lists of previous jobs and her mum's schooling. The names of two referees were there, her mum's last boss and her previous doctor.

She was about to turn to the last page when she saw something that made her stop.

PREVIOUS NAMES: Jill Peterson. She read it over again, unsure of what it meant. It was an odd question. Did it mean previous *married* name? Was it for people who were divorced, who had changed their name when they had remarried? But only their surname, surely?

Previous names: Jill Peterson.

Dear Jill, Just a line to let you know. . .

Had her mum once had a different name?

"Lou?" She heard Tommy's voice. "Might there be some big spiders in the bushes in the park?"

"There might," she said, her eyes still clinging to the name on the page, Jill Peterson. There were worry lines on her forehead and she began to tap at her teeth with her nails. *Jill Peterson*. It could have been a name that Anna used once to get a job, or a flat. It was a perfectly legal thing to do, no doubt about that. She would ask Anna when she came back.

After a few minutes of looking over the forms, she closed the file up and held it on her lap. She would simply ask Anna about it when she returned. It was a reasonable thing to ask, no one could deny that. Not even Anna.

"Lou, how many minutes, exactly, till we go to the park?" Tommy said.

"Soon as Mum comes back," she said, faltering for a moment in her words.

Anna Lewis. Jill Peterson.

Anna came back about twelve.

"It took longer than I thought," she said, crossly.

Lou said nothing but watched her as she unpacked her briefcase. She was wearing navy trousers and a cream shirt. Her badge was pinned on to the shirt pocket, *ANNA LEWIS PROJECT WORKER*. Around her neck was a light, chiffony scarf, different shades of deep pink, that Lou hadn't seen before.

"Was everything all right?" Anna said. "You're quiet. There wasn't any trouble, was there?"

"No," Lou said, looking away from Anna for a moment. On her lap was the Personnel file.

"Poor Sandra. She is terribly upset at having to move on," Anna said, taking some hand cream from a drawer and spurting it on to the backs of her hands.

"Oh."

It was a simple enough question, and it would only take a second or so to speak the words. Lou looked up, hugging herself, the file sitting precariously at the edge of her knees. She was about to speak when something stopped her. Anna had new earrings on. Long silver fringes that swayed gently every time she moved, sometimes touching the pink scarf with their tendrils. They gave Anna a kind of exotic look, like a gypsy. For an instant, just a few seconds, she didn't look like Anna at all, but some stranger that Lou didn't know.

"I. . ." Lou wanted to speak, but a sense of loss had taken hold of her as though Anna had gone and been replaced by someone else. Her knees must have twitched because the file that she had been holding had fallen on to the ground, and then she was on the floor picking it up and stuffing it back into the filing cabinet.

"What's that?" Anna's voice came from behind.

Lou turned, pulling all her strength together. *Who are you?* she wanted to say. *Who is Jill Peterson?*

The phone rang then. Like an alarm it cut a line between them, sharp and insistent, demanding to be answered. Anna picked it up and began to speak, crisp and business-like, and Lou knew that the moment had gone.

The past. It was a closed-up house. An old detached building with ornate iron trelliswork and leaded glass windows. Now there were some people trying to get out of it. Jill Peterson. The big woman at Brighton. The tiny girl in the sailor dress. At a big bay window, downstairs, was a giant rocking horse with brown eyes that seemed to swivel back and forth as she passed.

Lou took Tommy's hand and left the room while Anna was still speaking on the phone.

When the mums from the hostel were ready, Lou joined them to go to the park. It was just after two o'clock, and she saw several boys and girls of her own age hanging around the benches and gateways of the park, talking, laughing, pushing each other about playfully. She wondered if any of them were from the school she was due to go to. The uniforms were obscured, though, the colours blending into each other and she couldn't tell.

At the park Tommy played with some of the other boys in the sand. The mums she had gone with were deep in conversation with each other, their long cigarettes pointing into the distance, their eyes scanning the horizons of the park.

Lou looked at Tommy from time to time, and then at teenagers walking around the park, arm in arm, whispering secretly to each other. She remembered some of the girls she had made friends with: Kelly with the long red hair and Michelle whose brother worked in Burger King.

She suddenly felt very alone. A solitary figure on a bench in a park that seemed to spread for hundreds of miles.

She made herself think of Anna, of herself when she was a tiny child. In front of her eyes there was a hazy picture. It calmed her, made her feel soft and lazy.

Her mum was waiting at the school gates. It was her first day and she'd been in floods of tears. She'd been persuaded to go into the classroom because there'd been the promise of a toy on the way home. That day she'd got her toy: a nurse's set with a thermometer and a toy watch that hung upside down on her blouse. The tears had been just as strong the next morning and there had even been a promise then of something nice when she came out in the afternoon. It hadn't been such a good toy that time: a plastic doll whose arms and legs were rigid. The third day there'd been some impatience with the tears and a gentle shove past the classroom door. Lou had managed to swallow back the upset and had even liked the teacher who had given her a hug and a plastic box full of building bricks to play with.

In the afternoon there'd just been an ice cream.

It was the earliest memory she had. Before that there was just darkness, only the photo of her dad who had died when she was two.

Lou felt a stab of grief. It happened from time to time. She'd read an article about it in a women's magazine that she'd found in the hostel. She hadn't been aware, at the time, of her dad's death, so she hadn't been able to grieve for him then. The loss had come for her later, as she grew up, like stray bullets, hitting her unexpectedly. Her dad who she'd never known.

What about her mum? Anna? Did she really know her?

Jill Peterson. Had her mum changed her name after he had died? Did that mean that her dad's name had been Robert Peterson?

Sergeant Robert Peterson.

"Look, Lou!" Tommy's voice penetrated her thoughts. "See what we've made! It's a den!"

Lou looked. Tommy was in the middle of a small mountain of sand. His hair was covered and some of it was stuck to his glasses. She reached over, took them off his nose and started to rub them with a tissue.

"Here," she said, her heart as heavy as a bowling ball. "We'll have to go soon."

EIGHT

Two days later Lou broke the photograph frame. It was a shock. Finding out the truth about her dad.

The man she thought was her dad. Another one of Anna's lies.

"Tommy and me will do some housework today. Then we might go out to the park."

"Thanks, Lou," Ruth said. "You're so good with Tommy. He likes you such a lot. You should work with children when you leave school."

"Leave school!" Anna said. She was doing Ruth's hair, using both her hands to gather up the wiry mass and subdue it into a neatly woven plait at the base of her head. "Sometimes I think she's already left school. I don't know how she's going to get a job of any sort with the time she's missed."

"Mum!" Lou said. "I'm going on Monday!"

"So you say."

"I promise."

"It's my fault. She'd be at school now if it wasn't for Tommy," Ruth said.

"It's nothing to do with you, or Tommy. Lou's got this aversion to school. Whenever she can she'll try and avoid it. She's got a headache, stomach ache, earache. She's not done her homework; she's lost a book; some girls are being horrible to her, some girl is being too friendly with her and won't leave her alone."

"Mum!"

"On the other hand it might not be her fault. There's a teachers' training day; the boiler has broken down. It's the end of term so it's not worth going in on the last day. There's always a thousand reasons why Lou shouldn't be at school."

"That's not fair!" Lou said, in a hurt voice. She tried to keep a cross expression on her face but saw Ruth's hand over her mouth trying to hide a smile. Anna was weaving clumps of Ruth's hair in and out, holding on tightly as though they were the reins of a difficult horse.

"Next Monday, without fail," she said.

"I will," Lou said, her voice indignant.

"Tommy starts at the new child-minder's on Monday," Ruth said, giving Lou a wink, "and he'll finally start school in September."

"Um," she said. Tommy had been in nursery but hadn't been able to start school because of their moving about. Lou looked over at the little boy. He was playing with small figures on the floor. His lips were moving and he kept pushing his glasses up with his knuckles.

"Let's hope he likes it better than Lou does!" Anna said, standing back from Ruth's hair. "How's that?" she said.

Ruth got up and went across to the mirror.

"It's really nice, Anna, thanks," she said, and gave Anna a playful hug.

*

After they went, Lou sat Tommy in front of the TV and started to clear up.

It was an odd thing but Lou *liked* housework. She enjoyed seeing the pile of dirty dishes getting smaller and smaller, dripping dry on the draining board, and then being carefully wiped with a tea towel and replaced in a cupboard. It was nice to see everything in its place. A row of mugs upside down on the shelf; a pile of plates neatly stacked; knives, forks and spoons, each in their own compartment.

Anna hated housework, she freely admitted it.

"What I need is a wife!" she'd said mischievously, when Lou had complained about the unmade beds, the empty fridge, the grimy bathtub.

So Lou did it herself, grudgingly at first, but then got to like it.

The duvets were straightened, the towels hung out to dry, the floor swept and carpet vacuumed. All the while Tommy sat mesmerized by the TV and Lou found herself humming a tune, feeling a sense of satisfaction as every room began to look ordered, tidy, *settled*.

When she'd finished she sat down on one of the soft chairs and let a feeling of contentment wash over her. Glancing up she saw her dad's photo in the frame in the middle of the mantelpiece. She looked away purposely but her eyes were drawn back to it. She began to feel agitated, uneasy. While doing the housework her mind had seemed blank, at least only concerned with immediate things, the cleaning and the dusting.

Now, though, other things forced themselves into her head. She looked at Tommy who was curled up on the settee fingering the faded pillowcase that he called his Blanket. She put her legs up under her and after a few minutes let her thumb slip in between her lips while she gazed at breakfast TV.

In her head there was a list building up. The trip to Brighton, the rocking horse and the woman with the flowered dress. The photograph of the little girl in the sailor dress and the letter from Shoreham addressed to Jill. Now she had found out that her mum had once been called Jill Peterson.

These things niggled away at Lou. They were making everything untidy, out of place. Here she was with Anna, settled in a home and a job. For the first time she felt at ease, as though they weren't going to suddenly empty out the cupboards and drawers into cardboard boxes and black plastic bags.

But these other things, this list in her head wouldn't be put away, hung up, swept up, tidied into a cupboard.

Anna Lewis. Lou and Anna. They'd lived in lots of places together, slept in different bedrooms, moved around the country, sometimes in the middle of the night. Their life together had occasionally been chaotic. But at the heart of it there'd been this solidity, this giant post that Lou could hold on to whenever things got too difficult.

Lou tried to visualize what it was, this hard, tough thing that she'd leant against but all that ever came into her mind was the softness and warmth of Anna's skin; the smell of her perfume; the feel of her hair tickling Lou's neck or her metal earrings, cold on Lou's skin.

We're all right, aren't we, Lou?

And they had been.

Now, though, Anna was preoccupied with the hostel. Then there was Ruth. She had come home a couple of times and found Ruth cooking in the kitchen, or having a bath or reading a book. Anna seemed pleased at this, tasting Ruth's recipes and saying how nice they were. She didn't even seem to mind when Ruth had stayed the night a couple of times, even though she had her own room at the hostel. Lou *had* minded; finding Ruth's silk nightie draped across her mum's bed, she had screwed it up in a ball and shoved it in a carrier bag. Later, she had taken it out, folded it up and given it back to Ruth who had laughed and said, "Did I leave that old thing here?"

Anna seemed different now, since they had moved to this fiat. She hadn't even gone back to smoking. The unopened packet of cigarettes was still on the mantelpiece beside the framed picture of Lou's dad. They were both things from Anna's past. Lou felt a tinge of regret for this past, like a place on a map, that they were always moving away from.

She stood up and went across to the mantelpiece. The cigarettes were untouched. She plucked them out from behind the vase, moving it slightly. Turning away, the top of her arm must have caught the edge of the picture frame. She felt it move but could do nothing to stop it tumbling off the mantelpiece and hitting the stone fireplace surround below.

Tommy jumped when the crash came, looking up in alarm.

"Damn!" Lou said, looking at the dozens of pieces of glass glittering on the floor, the frame face down. "Tommy, don't walk about, there's glass everywhere here," and she replaced the cigarette packet and went to the kitchen to get the dustpan and brush.

Lou tutted to herself and gingerly stepped around the area of broken glass. She used a cushion to kneel down to pick up the bits. She took her time and swept up the ones that were too tiny for her to pick up. She would need to buy a new frame. She picked up the wooden surround and saw that the edge of the photo was coming out. It would be best to remove the whole thing.

She took it across to the table. In the back of her head she could hear the background music from the cartoon that Tommy was watching.

She expected the photograph to come out neatly but it didn't. She placed it face down and undid the catches from the back of the frame, lifting off the covering piece of cardboard.

She'd thought it would be a photograph. An oblong picture with a narrow white border.

But it wasn't. The paper was thin, like that in a magazine, and the edges were folded back.

She had a bad feeling inside her chest as she unfurled her dad's picture. It was a photograph of a soldier from a kind of Sunday newspaper supplement. The paper felt old, as though she might tear it easily if she wasn't careful. She spread the page out on the table, the photo of her dad, of Robert Lewis, in the bottom right hand corner of the page.

But it wasn't her dad at all. The caption underneath said, *Lieutenant George Samuel, killed in Northern Ireland, June 1985.*

Lou's eyes scanned it from corner to corner. She turned it over, read snatches from an article on the other side. All the time there was a rage growing inside her, prodding, pushing, pounding, at the insides of her chest. For years she had carried this photo around, looked after it, taken care of it as though it had been a physical part of her father. But it was a lie.

Her dad had died before 1985, when she was only two.

This had never been a photo of her dad. This had just been some picture that Anna had cut out of a magazine. Some story that she had made up.

Lou was aware of the music from the TV getting faster, gaining speed as though some cartoon character was being chased around. She held the picture in her hands, the one she had looked at a thousand times over the years, the one she had directed her emotions towards. The only thing she had left of her father, Sergeant Robert Lewis.

And it was a fake.

With her fingers she pulled the paper apart; doubling it up, she tore it again, letting the pieces flutter down on to the table. Then she closed her eyes and let her fists clench.

When she opened them Tommy was beside her.

"Look, Lou, you've made a mess," he said, pointing to the bits of paper lying scattered around her feet.

"Yes," she said. "I have."

NINE

It was only a few days later: Lou's first day at the comprehensive school, standing in her school uniform, waiting for Anna to leave for work. It was a dark green skirt and white blouse. There was a sweatshirt with a tiny crest on it but that was folded up in her brand new bag. She had black trainers on her feet and white socks.

It was like every other uniform she had ever had. Cheap polyester skirts with elasticated waists for growth; white shirt or polo shirt; stretchy sweatshirt, blue, green, black, the name of the school printed somewhere on it. Like a bag of flour, she was packed up and labelled and ready to go.

"You sure you're feeling all right?" Anna said. "You've been so quiet over the last few days. Even Ruth noticed. She said to me, what's up with Lou?"

"I've just been thinking about school."

"Well, you're going, so don't start the I-don't-feel-well performance!"

"I'm going, I've said I will!" Lou said, averting her eyes from Anna's face.

Anna came across to her. "It won't be so bad, honest. You'll see, within a few days you'll have some friends. I won't be able to stop you then!"

"Maybe," Lou said.

Friends. Adults seemed to think it was easy. It was as if

she was a puppy dog who would prick its ears and wag its tail and run off to play with the other dogs.

Lou gritted her teeth. Over the years she had made friends. There was Mary who had a passion for shopping; the two of them in and out of the malls, trying on skirts and jeans in Miss Selfridge. And then Suzy who had seven rabbits and four cats and who called them all by the names of famous people. They'd been sad when she had to leave, had wanted her to write. She'd said she would but Anna had said she couldn't.

Lou was hit by an ache of sadness, strong and overwhelming. It had to do with the friends she had lost over the years. She could have written, secretly, kept up a correspondence. Anna need never have known. But Lou couldn't lie to Anna; the thought of it had always made her feel edgy, unsettled. She couldn't live with such a lie even if Anna had never found out.

Anna had not had the same feelings. Anna had created a lie that they had lived with for years. A small finger of grief poked away at Lou's ribs and she had to close her eyes tightly for a few seconds.

"Here's some money for your lunch," Anna said, not noticing. She handed her a couple of pound coins. "I shan't be late this evening. Oh, Ruth will probably come for tea; you don't mind, do you?"

Lou took the money and shook her head. It didn't matter to her who came. If Ruth was there she didn't have to talk.

"I'll see you later, then." Anna kissed her on the cheek and walked out of the door.

Lou turned round to the mantelpiece. The space was there, in the middle, where her dad's photo had been. It had been gone for three days and her mum hadn't even noticed. All that was there was the unopened packet of cigarettes.

It was gone four when she got back home. In her bag were a number of new exercise books and a couple of text books. There was a timetable and a map of the school. She pulled them out and laid them across the table. They were firm proof that she'd gone, as she'd said she would.

Folded up inside one of the books was a form that had to be filled in by her mother. *Confidential Information* it said at the top. She'd filled in forms like it in every school she had ever gone to. It was full of the usual things: mother's name, father's name. Lou paused for a minute. Her mother would continue the lie and fill in the name of Robert Lewis. She felt her breath catch in her throat.

Had her father really been called Robert Lewis? Or Robert Peterson? Or was he just a man created by her mother? A false name, a photo taken from a magazine. A history that was made up. *He died in Northern Ireland, Lou. He was blown up by a bomb.*

How could she believe anything any more?

As a child, she had sat at Anna's feet, or cuddled up beside her on the armchair and she'd imagined her dad walking along a Belfast street. The houses were tiny and close together and at the end of each terrace there were giant murals on the wall, flags or pictures of men in face masks.

In her mind her dad had had a metal hat on his head and his rifle had been pointed nervously here and there.

He was just walking along the streets, Lou, and suddenly the bomb exploded.

Lou's mouth had made a tiny "o" whenever Anna said this. In her mind she had pictured him stepping gingerly down the street. The bomb had been there clearly in front of him; she had visualized it rather like one of the mines that float in the sea, a black round thing with spikes coming out of it. Her dad had put one foot in front of the other, somehow not seeing the bomb that was sitting there.

The explosion blew the windows out of all the houses and killed another two people along with your dad, Lou.

Had the explosion been like an enormous firework? A deafening sound? Had there been smoke and splinters of glass flying, like darts, through the air?

Somehow her dad, who had been walking along the street, wasn't there any more. There had just been a space in the picture in Lou's mind.

And it was all a lie.

Lou looked at the confidential form in front of her and felt her chest tighten.

Was it the only lie that her mother had told her?

Over the last few days, possibly even before she had seen the picture in the magazine, something unpleasant had been forming itself in Lou's mind.

It was like a kind of collage; bits of pictures here and there, some words even: Anna's other name, the rocking horse, the big lady in the flowered dress, holding the little girl's hand. These things seemed to be pasted on to some flat sheet. Moments later, though, it would change and become cylindrical and seemed to turn into itself like a kaleidoscope, one picture turning into the other.

Anna had lied about her dad; Lou had no idea why.

She had a strong memory of another woman who was with her when she was very young, of a trip to Brighton.

Was Anna her *real* mother?

This question had sent Lou into a mild panic. She had had to sit very still and breathe deeply while she let the idea float about inside her head.

Could she have been adopted?

The big lady in the flowered dress, was *she* her real mother? Had she died? Had Anna (or Jill) adopted her?

The pictures in her head continued to move but this time it was like a roll of film that was uncurling, the images all in a straight line, as if they'd been shuffled up and put in chronological order.

The big lady, Sally, had been Lou's real mother. It was she who had died (not her dad) and Anna had taken care of her.

Anna was her adopted mother.

This wasn't such an awful thought; it explained many of the things that had happened over the last weeks. It only meant that Anna wasn't her *biological* mother. She was her *real* mother in every other way.

But why hadn't she told her? Been honest with her?

*

Lou spread the form out on the table and began to fill it in. That was when she had the idea. The solution that would clear the mystery up once and for all.

Date of Birth it had said on the form, and she'd filled the numbers in without even thinking about it.

Her date of birth was on her birth certificate. If she could see that it would state clearly who her real mother was (and her real father).

It would be in black and white.

She stood up, letting the form drop out of her hand, and went towards Anna's bedroom, towards the box file that held the personal papers. All she had to do was sort through and find her birth certificate. It would clear up the uncertainty. She knelt down and pulled the box from under Anna's bed and smiled at the crooked writing on the top and the misspelt word, PESONAL PAPERS. She'd had a felt tip and written it on one afternoon while Anna had been tidying it up. She'd left the "r" out of personal but Anna had said it didn't matter, as long as they knew what was in the box. *What's spelling between friends?* Anna had said.

Lou opened the box and with both hands lifted the contents out: a pile of papers about eight centimetres thick.

She would sort through the papers and find her birth certificate. Then the uncertainty would be gone.

It was almost six o'clock and Lou was still sitting on the bedroom floor. Scattered around her were papers and documents from the box.

She'd not found her birth certificate but in her hand there was something else. She read it over and over again, each time being stung further by the words and the headline. From time to time she let it fall from her fingers and rest on the carpet but then she snatched it up again, her eyes eating up the words on the paper, her thoughts spinning with nausea.

She wasn't Anna's daughter at all; she'd been right to think that.

In her hand was a newspaper article. It was from the front page of the *Shoreham Weekly Recorder*. There was no date but the paper was old, yellowing. The article read:

CHILD SNATCHED WHILE MOTHER IS SHOPPING
Two-year-old Louise Robinson was stolen from her mother in Jubilee Precinct. The toddler was asleep in her pushchair while her mother, Sally Robinson, was in the chemist's. "I only left her for a minute," a distraught Mrs Robinson said. "She was asleep and I didn't want to wake her up. I only had a prescription to get."

Police are looking for a young woman who was seen hurrying away from the scene with a pushchair. Several passers-by said that she was in her mid-twenties with dark hair that was covered up with a headscarf.

The sound of the key in the front door made Lou sit up. She looked round at the mess on the floor.

"Lou, I'm back!" She heard Anna's voice.

She folded the article and pushed it into her skirt pocket,

then scooped up the rest of the papers and pushed them quickly back into the box.

"How was school?" the voice continued.

She stood up and shoved the box under the bed with her foot just as Anna came into the room.

"Hello, love. How was it today?"

"Fine," Lou said, her hand over her pocket where the article was.

"There. I told you it wouldn't be so bad!"

"Yes," Lou said.

Later, after Ruth and Tommy had gone, Lou looked at the article over and over again. Sally Robinson was her real mother.

Anna Lewis had stolen her.

TEN

Afterwards, Lou could never quite remember how she'd spent the days that followed. In her memory they were a blur; the pictures were off focus, crackled like a faulty TV screen. There were several blacked-out moments and some periods when she'd seemed like an automaton, getting up, going to school, coming home, washing the dishes, watching the telly, going to bed.

"You're very quiet," Anna had said several times.

"You've not got much to say for yourself," Anna had said on her way out to the pictures with Ruth.

"Honestly, Lou, what's eating you?" Anna had said across the breakfast table.

The one thing she did remember was hiding the evidence.

When Anna was working late one evening she'd laid it all on the table in front of her: the photo and the letter, the newspaper cutting. The man's picture from the frame she had already thrown away in tiny pieces. Beside these things, invisible and intangible, were her memories of Brighton, of the big woman in the flowered dress, her real mother.

She looked at it all for a while. In her mind she named each of the items, exhibit one, two, etc., the way she'd seen it done in TV programmes featuring courtroom scenes.

For that's what it was. Evidence against Anna Lewis who

had stolen her from her real mum. Anna Lewis who used to be Jill Peterson. Lou sat back and thought about the day that it had happened.

Her real mum, Sally, had tucked her up in her pushchair. She had maybe kissed her quickly on the head and then walked out, pushing her to the shops. Along the way she may have talked softly to her. "*Look at the birds, Lou. There's a big truck. Look at the man drilling the road, Lou. . .*"

Jill Peterson had been a friend of her real mother's. She had known her for a number of years; the letter certainly made it sound like that. Yet she had come to Shoreham on that day and stolen her from Sally. Could it be that she had been desperate for a child of her own? Had she lost a child, in a miscarriage or a still birth?

At this point Lou had stopped and swept up the items on the table in front her as though they were a hand of cards.

She always stopped thinking about it when she began to feel sorry for Anna. Instead of the hardness and fury inside her chest there was a sort of hollowing, as if her insides had shrunk back. She could almost feel a space there, a great dark hole which only closed up when she made herself think in an angry way.

She had a mum and dad who hadn't seen her for thirteen years. That was Anna's fault. Lou began to lay out the bits of paper and photograph again, looking at them and letting the hurt build up inside her throat.

Jill had been childless. She had been friendly with Sally,

her mother, who had said in her letter to her that she was expecting another child. It wasn't fair that Jill couldn't have a baby when Sally evidently had no problems.

That's why Lou had gone to Jill without any problem. She had known her, had seen her as a familiar, friendly face.

Jill had taken the pushchair from outside the chemist's shop. She had probably said something soothing. "*Look, Lou, it's Jill. Remember me? There's a good girl! Look at the doggie, Lou. . .*" She had a whole new wardrobe of clothes for the child, had dressed her up and taken her off on the first train to London. She had made up a new name, Anna Lewis, and taken a train to the north of England, where they had spent a number of years moving around.

Lou had become Anna's baby, had grown to love her, to see her as her mother.

Until the day that she had found the newspaper cutting.

The rest – the lie about her dad, the mystery and false name – now all made sense. They added up to something. *Anna was not her real mother*.

Part of Lou wanted to take the pieces of paper and photograph and tear them into tiny pieces, or take a match and set them alight, watching them curl and disintegrate into black ash, so that they disappeared as though they had never existed. That would be another lie, though, to pretend it hadn't happened. To deny that she had a real mum and dad somewhere.

Instead she decided to bury them.

She found some brown paper bags and newspaper. She

began by placing the photo of the child in the middle. She wrapped this up inside the letter and the newspaper article. She put these inside the paper bag and that inside another. She didn't look at the clock but she felt the minutes tick slowly past as she folded and wrapped and covered and packed.

She was left with a parcel the size of a small shoebox.

She was reminded of a similar sized parcel that Anna had given her a couple of Christmases ago. She'd smiled, holding it in her hands, but she'd felt disappointment like a ton weight on her shoulders. For Christmas she'd wanted a particular jacket. She'd hinted and pointedly tried it on when they were out shopping. She'd said what colour she'd wanted it in and specified the size she would buy if she had the money. She'd been so sure that it would be bought as a Christmas present for her. She'd taken the wrapped present, a little bigger than a shoebox, and smiled cheerfully while opening it. Layer upon layer of coloured Christmas paper had peeled off until finally there'd been a tiny box, the kind that jewellery was usually packed in.

Lou had pushed away the crumpled up paper and taken the lid off the box, expecting some earrings.

Instead, there'd been a small card which she'd opened. Inside the words had said, *Look in my wardrobe*. She'd run out of the room and down the hall and flung open the tiny wardrobe door. There, hanging in a plastic cover, was the jacket that she had wanted. Outside the room she heard Anna laughing. *"Your face!"* she kept repeating. *"Your face!"*

This time the package held no surprises for her.

Lou took it and put it under a pile of clothes in her drawer. She closed the drawer tightly and sat on the bed looking at it. As long as it was there, covered, hidden, she wouldn't be bothered with it. It had to stay there firmly in the drawer, out of sight.

Maybe she could forget about it. She laughed at the thought of this. As if she could continue with her daily life as though the items, the exhibits, the *evidence* had never existed.

Because there was always the police to think about.

Anna had committed an offence, a dreadful crime. If Lou were to take the things she had found to the police, what would happen? Anna would be put in prison and Lou would be reunited with her real mum and dad.

Sometimes that thought made her happy, made her feel righteous, revenged. Then later she would think of Anna, inside a brick-walled cell, sitting on a bed, looking round with incomprehension. Maybe she would cry and say "*I didn't mean to do it.*"

The thought made Lou weak and for a moment she felt as though her eyes would dissolve in water. She swallowed a few times but her saliva was sharp and her throat felt grazed. She couldn't go to the police, she couldn't.

Sometimes during those first few days Lou thought she might go mad with worry about it all.

She might well have done if it hadn't been for Charlie Short.

PART TWO

ELEVEN

Lou had never heard Charlie's surname before.

She was helping him fix a broken window in the attic when she found out.

He stood there before her like a giant in the tiny room, his shoulders bent so that his head would not touch the ceiling. The light fitting was still swinging gently where his arm had hit it. . .

Charlie Short.

Amid all the misery that she felt she'd just started laughing. "Charlie *Short*," she'd said, pointing up at him. "*Charlie Short!*"

"All right, Lulu," he said. "That's original. No one's ever said that to me before."

But she couldn't stop laughing.

"Couldn't you have changed your name?" she said.

He turned away and put his arm up across his eyes. In a muffled voice he said, "I'm sorry but I've got a thing about my height. It's always been a problem for me."

"Oh," she said, the laughter stopping abruptly. The feelings of delight seemed to drain out of her in a moment. He was hurt. She had hurt his feelings.

"I'm sorry, Charlie," she said, moving towards him, "I'm really sorry."

His shoulders began to shake.

"Honestly, Charlie, I didn't mean. . ." She put her hand on his arm.

He turned round and his eyes were crinkled and his mouth was open. He was laughing. He grabbed her wrist and held it.

"You!" she said and started laughing again. "Charlie Tall," she said.

"We're going to continue this then, are we, Miss Louise Misery?" he said. "Or Miss Louise Moody."

"There's no need to be like that," she said, turning away, her anger rising quickly.

"Now, now," he pulled her back by the shoulder, his hand sliding down to the top of her arm. "It was only a joke."

"You can take a joke too far," she said, softening.

He picked up her hand. She could feel the hard skin on his fingers.

"How about this one, Lulu Gorgeous?" he said, raising his eyebrows. He let go of her hand and ruffled her hair. Then he bent down to his tool box.

"My name is *Lou*. I've told you!" She said it half-heartedly though, turning away with sudden shyness. Her hair was ruffled where he had messed it up but she hardly liked to smooth it down again. He was kneeling on the floor and his head, his hair, was inches away from her. It was dark brown, wiry, not unlike Ruth's. It was pulled back tightly into a band at the back of his neck. Even if she had put her fingers into it she could not have moved it. At the base of his neck the hair seemed to explode out of the band. She had an urge to reach across and touch it.

She looked at his profile. He was singing a silent song, his lips moving but no sound coming out. She looked at his hands, sorting through the box. His forefingers were pointing directly out front, like tiny drumsticks, they were hitting some invisible drum.

"First week at school over then, Lou," he said. He'd stopped singing, perhaps come to the end of the song. His forehead was creased. He was concentrating, sorting through a box of tiny nails that looked like dressmaking pins.

"Yes," she said.

"How was it?"

"Not so terrible."

"I told you."

"Um. . ." Lou sat down on the floor. She crossed her legs and leaned back against the wall. On the floor was a piece of glass that Charlie was going to fit into the frame.

"Where did you go to school?"

"Here and there," he said. "We moved around a lot, my family."

"Did you?" Lou said. "Same as me and . . . and Anna." She was going to say "Mum" but she was trying to stop herself using the word. Anna thought it was funny. Lou had overheard her saying to Ruth the previous day, "*Lou's going through an independent phase at the moment. She hardly ever calls me Mum any more.*" Lou felt her neck harden momentarily at the thought of Anna. She rubbed at it with her fingers.

"My dad's in the building trade. He moved where the

work was. We lived up north for a while. And on the south coast. Then round London."

"You live with your parents?"

"No. No, I'm staying with a mate at the moment. My parents moved back down to the coast. I stayed on in London. In October I'll go back to university."

"University?" Lou said.

"Don't you think I'm brainy enough?" Charlie said, picking up a small ball of putty that looked like Blu-Tack.

"No, I don't mean that," Lou started to say but her words faltered. She hadn't thought of Charlie like that. She couldn't imagine him with his nose in a book.

"I know. Charlie's a builder. He must be thick."

"No," Lou said. He was right in a way.

"I'm in the second year of my degree. It's good. I'm enjoying it."

He looked directly at her. His eyes seemed to move across her face and then down her neck to her chest. Then he looked back to the piece of glass. 'Want to help me here or not?" he said.

She stood up and he handed her the tiny nails, about a dozen of them.

"Right, Lulu, you hand me those and we'll have this window done in no time."

Later, when she went down to the office, Anna was there.

"Hi, Lou," she said. She was dialling a number on the phone, using her middle finger to jab at the buttons. "Where've you been?"

"Helping Charlie." She said the words dully, without interest.

Anna stopped dialling and replaced the phone receiver.

"Is there something wrong, Lou? You've been really low lately."

"Nope," Lou said.

"It's that school, isn't it?" Anna went on. "You don't like it. You're punishing me for sending you."

"No," Lou said, truthfully.

"You've got to go to school. That's the law. It's not my fault. I was only saying to Ruth the other day, Lou acts as if I, personally, am responsible for the whole school system."

Lou rolled her eyes at the mention of Ruth's name. Ruth this, Ruth that. Was there anything in their lives now that Ruth wasn't a part of?

"What's the matter? Why are you making that face? Is it that you don't like Ruth? Ruth's a friend. Surely you don't mind me having a friend?"

"No, I don't," Lou said.

Anna got up and walked around the desk. She walked up to Lou and put her arm around her shoulder. Lou could smell her perfume and feel her hair on the side of her face. Anna's arm gripped hers, rubbing it up and down. She was reminded of Charlie's touch, his calloused fingers on her hand.

"Cheer up, Lou. What's the matter? You can tell me."

Lou felt herself softening. How nice it would be to slump into Anna's arms and forget all the stuff that she had found out! She felt her legs bending and her hands curling, her neck leaning towards the soft shoulder.

But it was no good.

She had to be hard. She straightened her back and clenched her fists and said, "I want to know where my dad is buried."

Anna stood absolutely still, her eyes boring through Lou, her forehead crinkling up.

"What do you mean? I've told you, that's in the past."

"For you it is. For me it isn't," Lou said, her words croaky.

"This is all about me and Ruth, isn't it?"

"No."

"It is. It is! Whenever I've had a boyfriend you've always made me pay for it! Always. Now that Ruth and I are close, you don't like it."

"Its not about RUTH," Lou said, her words loud. Why did her mum insist on thinking the wrong thing? "It's about my DAD," she said and added, softly, "It's about me and my dad."

Anna looked away, her lips tightly shut together. Then the office door burst open and Tommy came running in.

"Lou! Lou! I'm going swimming," he said. Ruth was behind him.

"Why don't you come, Lou?" she said. Her hair was pulled up on top of her head in a tight bun. Some loose bits fell down from the back and curled around her neck.

Lou looked away from her towards Anna and then closed her eyes.

"No thanks, I'm helping Charlie," she said, and walked across the room and out of the door.

Charlie was in the garden fixing a drainpipe that had come away from the wall.

A few of the women were sitting on deck chairs down at the far end of the lawn. They had set up a small paddling pool that some of the toddlers were jumping in and out of.

"Hold this up for me, will you, Lou?" he said.

It was a warm afternoon and she was feeling tired. Charlie was hot, too. He had rolled his sleeves up to his shoulders and his face looked red. She didn't feel like doing anything but she did anyway. She stretched her arms up and pushed the pipe against the brick wall.

"I'm going to drill these holes quite close to you, Lou, but don't worry, I'm a good aim."

Lou smiled. Charlie was centimetres away from her. She stood rigidly still, holding the pipe securely, concentrating on what she was doing, waiting for the drill to pierce the quiet of the afternoon. After a few seconds she looked round. Charlie wasn't getting the drill ready at all. He was looking at her.

"What's wrong?" she said, self-conscious, her arms in the air.

He said nothing, just stood still. She felt his gaze as though it was something physical, an invisible touch.

"Charlie, hurry up, my arms are getting tired," she said, flustered, embarrassed.

"Hold your horses, I'm just fixing the correct drill bit in place."

The drill was only inches away but it felt like it was inside her rib cage. She closed her eyes tightly but it seemed to pierce her forehead and make her nerve ends vibrate and tremble.

When it was over she lay back on the grass. Charlie squatted down beside her, packing away the drill attachments.

"What are your parents like?" she said, thinking of Anna.

"They're all right," he said. "My mum fusses a bit and my dad's always slipping me a couple of quid for a burger and a drink. I don't think they realize that I'm nearly twenty!"

"Do you see them often?"

"Now and then. I get in the van and go down to the coast."

"Where do they live?" Lou said.

"Near Brighton. Just a couple of miles outside. It's all retirement homes and bowls but the beach is nice."

Brighton. Lou sat up, thinking of the tiny streets creeping away from the sea front. She remembered looking out to sea at the broken pier, its middle section bitten off and spat out by the sea.

"I like Brighton," she said.

"Tell you what." Charlie was standing up. "I was thinking of going down there next weekend. Why don't you come with me? Ask Anna. I'll look after you."

Charlie turned away and walked back to the house. Lou stood up and hurried after him through the kitchen and out of the front door. Along the way he picked up a couple of bags and a box of chisels.

"I'm working away all next week. I'm helping a mate of Arthur's at a job in south London. Tell Anna I won't be around."

She went to his van and helped him pack his stuff. She wanted to say something about Brighton but she couldn't. He was mouthing a song and seemed to have forgotten.

"I'll definitely come to Brighton." She blurted the words out.

"OK," he said.

Looking up for a moment she saw Anna's face at the window. Charlie looked up at the same moment. He raised his hand to wave but her mum had moved back, out of the way.

"Ring me in the week and I'll let you know what time, Lulu," he said, and put his hand on her hair, messing it up again.

"I'm definitely coming," she said, watching the van drive away down the street. There was a feeling of elation, like a fizzy drink, bubbling away in her chest.

TWELVE

Anna was adamant that Lou shouldn't go to Brighton.

"It's very nice of Charlie to ask but you can't go and that's an end to it. He's too old for you, Lou. I can't have you going off for the day with a young man of his age." Her words were precise and clipped. She was in her office, going through a folder of papers. Lou watched her with mounting frustration.

"His parents live down there. It's just a day out."

"Lou, I don't mind you having a boyfriend, but he's too old!"

"He's not a boyfriend," Lou said, almost believing it herself.

"You're not going. That's my final word, Lou."

Lou was in love.

She hadn't known it as that early on. At first she'd just been excited by Charlie's interest in her.

He was interested in her, she was sure.

She'd rushed home after he'd left and stood looking in her bedroom mirror. She looked at her fair hair, cut short at the back but longer round the sides. Her face was thin, worried-looking; with make-up she could look better, *older* even. She was skinny, though, with hardly any breasts at all.

Charlie had seen her at her worst, however. He had still called her "Gorgeous". As a joke to start off with, but then there were the long looks she'd had from him and the touch of his hand on her arm, on her hand.

She sat on the edge of the bed and let herself be drawn back, trance-like, to the moment when he'd been looking at her in the garden. His eyes had been like fingers tracing a pattern across her body. She felt a mild shiver at her neck.

He did like her, she was sure. Wasn't she?

She opened her wardrobe and pulled out clothes: a long skirt, a pair of jeans, some shorts. She held the dress in front of her. Would it be too formal for a day out? Would she be better in shorts and a T-shirt? She opened her drawers and looked for a top. She pulled out a couple of old ones that had lost their shape and some of their colour. Underneath, her hand touched the parcel of evidence that she had hidden away, wrapped up like a birthday present. She stopped and looked at it for a moment and realized that for a few hours, for a while, she hadn't been upset by it at all.

Maybe she had even forgotten it.

She pushed it back underneath the clothes and shut the drawer tightly. If it stayed there, out of sight, there was a chance that she could ignore it, at least for a while.

She held the dress in front of her again, glancing from time to time at the closed drawer. She picked up the shorts. She couldn't decide. She lay on her bed. After a few minutes she put her thumb into her mouth and began to suck it gently.

*

She wouldn't have called it *love*.

Not until Anna had said she couldn't go to Brighton with him.

Until then she couldn't have put a name to her feeling. It was as if she were a lit firework, waiting to go off. She was choking with anticipation, agitated a lot of the time, jumpy, tensing at the slightest noise or loud voice. Every now and then, for no apparent reason, her face broke into a smile like a half moon.

Anna had been oblivious. She had said "no" even though Lou had tried to be really nice, had called her "Mum" a couple of times.

"He's too old, Lou. At least for you he is! You're just not going and that's the end of it."

But it hadn't been the end of it. It had been the beginning. A powerful feeling had taken hold of Lou; it was as if there'd been an implosion, her emotions thrusting up inside her chest.

"You're too young to spend a whole day with a young man that you hardly know," Anna had said, slamming the drawer of the filing cabinet shut.

Lou couldn't have spoken even if she'd wanted to.

She left the hostel with a swooning feeling in her head. She walked round the corner to the flat. She thought of Charlie and his ponytail, his hand ruffling her hair. She imagined him in some other place, fixing a shelf or measuring up a door frame, other people around him, making cups of tea. Maybe there was someone there he would call "Gorgeous". She stopped walking and leaned up against the wall, a sudden feeling of loss gripping her. What if she were never to see him again?

She pulled herself together and walked on to the flat.

She was going to go to Brighton, whatever Anna said.

On Wednesday evening she phoned Charlie.

"Hello, Lulu," he said. He sounded sleepy.

"Anna says I can go to Brighton with you."

"OK, I'll pick you up. . ."

'No, don't do that. Anna works late on Friday night and I don't want to wake her. Why don't you pick me up at the bottom of the street, say about seven. . ."

She put the phone down and walked away.

On Thursday evening Ruth and Tommy came round.

Lou watched as Ruth gave Anna a kiss on the cheek and a hug that seemed to last for a long time. Ruth's hair was pulled back into a ponytail, the way Charlie wore his. It was the same kind of hair as well, thick, difficult to manage. Lou watched as Anna gave the ponytail a playful tug and then bent down to pick up Tommy.

Ruth turned to Lou and said, "How are you? How's the dreaded school been this week?"

"OK," Lou said.

"Guess what?" Anna said. "Lou's got herself a Saturday job down the market, on a stall."

"That's good, selling what?"

"Spices and things," Lou said, brightly, with forced enthusiasm.

"She'll be earning her own money. At last. What every parent longs for," Anna said, laughing.

"How long till you earn some money, Tommy?" Ruth gave Tommy a hug.

"Can I come, Lou?" Tommy said.

"No." Lou forced a smile. "It's a very early start. I've got to be there by seven!"

"Make sure you get paid overtime," Ruth said.

Lou smiled and looked at the three of them. Ruth was sitting on the settee holding Tommy on her lap and Anna was sitting beside her.

It looked like a pose for a family photograph.

THIRTEEN

Brighton was hot and full of traffic.

They parked the car in an underground car park and walked along the front.

"I'm glad Anna let you come," Charlie said. He had to lower his head to speak to her. She had to go on tiptoe to hear what he said.

"She's got a lot on her mind." Lou almost shouted to be heard above the sound of revving engines and snapping horns.

"It's not a job I'd like," he said, stopping at the edge of the road to wait for a gap in the cars.

"She *loves* it," Lou said, remembering Anna's delighted smile when she got the phone call confirming the job.

She'd been pacing all afternoon, waiting for news. When the phone had rung she'd reached her hand out two, maybe three times, to pick up the receiver. She'd held back though and counted to five before calmly picking the handset up and saying the number. "That's good news," she'd said, her voice even, flat. "I'd be delighted to accept the post." She'd been silently stamping her foot, though, her free arm up in the air as though she were a pupil asking a question. When she put the phone down she did a complete revolution and said, "I've got it! I've got it!" as if she'd just won the lottery.

The traffic was heavy, exhaust fumes curling up into the air that they were breathing. Lou was squinting her eyes because of the sun when she felt Charlie grab her hand and pull her across the road. When they got to the other side he didn't let it go but walked on, her hand in his, on to the wooden pier.

She said nothing but inside she felt a silent shiver. *He's holding my hand!* She had to quicken her steps to keep up with his long strides and for a moment she saw a mental picture of the two of them, not unlike a little girl out for the day with her father.

"Come on, slowcoach. I want to go right to the end of the pier."

They walked through the funfair and rides, past the fortune teller and rock and souvenir shops. They got to the point where a number of men were leaning over the handrail of the pier, holding long thin rods that hung down delicately into the brown sea sloshing about below. Lou looked through the gaps between the wooden beams and saw it beneath her, dark and jelly-like.

When they got to the very end there were more men fishing, their elbows casually on the barrier, their rods reaching into the air, the seagulls dive-bombing around them.

"Here we are, Gorgeous," Charlie said and pulled her on to a bench that faced the open sea. "Look at that. Miles and miles of nobody."

Lou looked, her hand making a shelf above her eyes to block out the sun.

"At least there's no traffic here," Charlie said.

He'd stopped holding her hand but they were sitting close, her leg touching his. They were about the same height too, Charlie just a few inches taller than her.

"Look," she said, turning to him. "I'm nearly as tall as you are."

He turned and looked straight at her. She was embarrassed for a moment by his unswerving attention. She was about to turn away, to point to something out at sea, to break his attention, when he lifted his hand and pulled her face towards him.

She'd been kissed before, by a boy she'd been friendly with in her previous school. They'd gone to the pictures and his mouth had wetly covered hers all evening. After every kiss she'd used the back of her hand to wipe away the dampness.

Charlie's mouth hardly seemed to touch hers at all. He turned his head to the side and his tongue slid along her teeth and then into her mouth. She had closed her eyes and opened her lips but her hands had stayed in her lap, gripping each other with tension.

He was holding her shoulders and his hand slid down her arm on to her elbow. He pulled back for a moment and said, "Relax, Lulu. This is meant to be nice."

She found herself smiling and let her hands unlock, finally lifting one of them up to his face and stroking his skin. Then he kissed her again, harder, his hand in her hair, his breathing becoming laboured, his mouth moving from side to side.

After a while he stopped and they sat with their backs against the bench, looking out to sea. One or two of the fishermen seemed to be looking at them.

Lou didn't care. Her lips were slightly open, her skin still tingling from his fingers, her breathing quick, as though she'd just been running. She screwed her eyes up and looked into the sun.

"Hey," he said after a minute. "I think we should get you some shades. Come on." He pulled her up by the hand, back along the pier, his long legs taking giant steps along the rickety wooden floor.

He bought her a pair of sunglasses in a shop by the front. She wanted to give him a thank you kiss for them. She stood on her toes and puckered her lips. After laughing and looking round, he let her kiss him. He seemed embarrassed in front of everyone. She felt a momentary flash of disappointment but then he said, "You look great in those, Lou," and they walked on, past the groups of kids who hung around the arcades, towards the shops for lunch.

She sat down in the café while Charlie went up to the counter to order the food. For the first time in ages she thought of Anna. She looked at her watch. It was one-fifteen. She would phone her about four and say that she was going for a coffee after work with a friend from school.

Anna was going out to a concert with Ruth and Tommy. She wouldn't be back until about ten. As long as Lou and

Charlie got back before then she should be all right. There would be no trouble.

Not that Lou cared. That's what she told herself. If Anna wanted to shout at her or ground her, or punish her in some way it was up to her. It wasn't as if she were her *real* mum. She could rant and rave all she liked, cry even, if she wanted, and Lou wouldn't care.

But Lou did care. Any picture of Anna crying threw Lou into a confused state, gave her a lump in her throat, made her want to reach out and touch Anna. She took her sunglasses off and rubbed the top of her nose.

There would be no crying, though, because Anna thought Lou was at work; in any case she was busy at the hostel and going out with Ruth and Tommy in the evening.

Lou opened her bag to put the sunglasses away. Inside was her address book. She flicked through it. On the back page was the address she had copied from the letter she'd found weeks before in Anna's old bag: *The Tulips, Swallow Drive, Shoreham.*

Charlie came back with the tray and put the food on the table. Lou picked a chip absentmindedly off her plate.

"Charlie, I've got some relatives in a place near here, Shoreham. Is that anywhere near where your mum and dad live?"

"A couple of miles further on," he said, sprinkling vinegar on to his plate. "Why, do you want to drop in on them?"

"I'm not sure," Lou said. "I don't know, maybe."

*

By the time they'd got out of the car park the crowds were dense on the pavements and spilling over on to the road. The traffic was moving in spurts. Charlie had the radio on and was singing along with a song. Every few seconds he played an imaginary instrument of some kind, the drums, the guitar, finally picking up a Mars bar he'd bought and using it as a mouth organ.

Lou looked at his profile, his ponytail tight at the back of his neck, his T-shirt cut away at the sleeves, showing his muscular arms. She felt a kind of wonder at him. She wanted to reach over and stroke his arms, let her fingers comb through his hair. She didn't though. She was suddenly shy and for a moment unsure as to why she was there. She looked out of the van window and saw only older, stylish women walking by in tight shorts and T-shirts. She looked down at herself, her old dress, her flat chest. *What does he see in me?* she said to herself. The road finally cleared when they were a mile or so outside Brighton. He turned the sound of the radio up loud and she slipped her shoes off and put her bare feet up on the dashboard.

When there was a gap in the music he said, "I'll spend about an hour or so with my mum and dad, then I'll pick you up on the corner of Swallow Drive, say about four. Then we'll make our way back to London. We can stop on the way for a pizza or something. What do you think?"

"Yep," Lou said, her confidence draining out of her. It wasn't a good idea to go to Shoreham. She felt a mild panic in her throat. What was she going to do? Go and find her real mum and introduce herself? She opened her mouth to say something but realized that the car was slowing down. It stopped within view of a sign that said *Welcome to Shoreham*.

"Here we are," he said, and she closed her mouth. She would look stupid if she changed her mind without any explanation. He leaned across and kissed her gently on the lips. "See you later," he said, and she stepped out on to the pavement and watched him drive away.

FOURTEEN

She phoned Anna first, then walked along the main street. It wasn't as crowded as Brighton but there were people browsing in the shops and adults and children walking along, talking excitedly, heading for the sea. It took her just over ten minutes to walk from one end of the place to the other. When she found herself retracing her steps she stopped and looked at her watch. She had an hour or so to kill before Charlie came back. She saw a café and decided to wait out the time in there.

She sat down and drank a cup of strong tea and looked through the window at the surrounding shops.

Why had she come? She had decided, two weeks ago, that there was nothing she could do about the things she had found out. What was the point of coming here, to the place where she thought her real mother lived?

If she approached her, said, *I'm the daughter that was stolen from you*, what would happen to Anna? She looked down into her teacup and saw police officers and solicitors and barristers. She saw the bare walls of a cell. She imagined Anna, on a worn mattress, in a grey shapeless dress. Her knees would be up on the bed and she would be hugging them with her arms. She would have a bewildered expression on her face.

Perhaps Anna hadn't thought she was doing anything wrong?

Lou sat up because something had occurred to her. Perhaps Anna took Lou because she didn't like the way she was being treated; thought, in fact, that she was unloved, uncared for.

But then she remembered Brighton and the big soft lady whose dress had flapped around her face, the little girl in the sailor dress skipping along the Lanes.

Lou had good memories of the day at Brighton and the woman. She was just clutching at straws.

She went back to looking out through the café window at the people walking past. After a few seconds her eye caught a sign on a brick wall: Jubilee Precinct. It was a small square courtyard on the other side of the road. There were four shops in it: a delicatessen, an antique shop, a flower shop and a chemist.

Lou remembered the newspaper article. The little girl had been stolen from outside a chemist's in Jubilee Precinct. "I only left her for a minute," were the mother's words.

She drank her tea and got up to pay.

Outside she walked across the road to the precinct. It was small, the size of a tennis court. It was paved with uneven stones and in the middle there was a raised flower bed. Beside it was a pushchair with a sleeping child, its arm hanging out the side, its mouth open, around its neck a dummy on a piece of ribbon.

This was where Lou had been taken from.

On the wall by the delicatessen there was a map of the town, in the middle an arrow that said YOU ARE HERE. Lou looked at it, her eyes scanning from one side of the paper to the other. *The Tulips*, *Swallow Drive*, *Shoreham*. She found the road in just a few seconds.

Lou turned into Swallow Drive and stood very still for a moment, looking it up and down. The houses were on one side only. Across the way was an old church, its front lawn sloping down to meet the pavement. Lou could see about a dozen houses before the road twisted away, out of her sight.

Although she was still, her feet anchored to the ground, she felt her heart thudding insistently, as if she'd been jogging and had come to the end of a run. Lou knew this road. With firm certainty she knew she'd been to this place before.

There was a bench by the cobbled wall that ran outside the church. She walked across and sat on it, opening her bag to get the sunglasses out and put them on.

It was very hot and she closed her eyes behind the dark lenses and searched back into her memory to visualize the houses. In her mind's eye they were as tall as the sky. She had to push her head back to see the pointed roofs and the tops of the trees. The fences and walls were far above her and the gates were huge and heavy to push open. Turning to the road she saw the church on the other side very far away, another world, the flat stones of the graveyard peeping mysteriously from behind the uneven wall. A giant car whooshed past her and in her head she heard the words, "*Careful, Lou, don't go too close to the road.*"

Lou opened her eyes and let them linger from house to house until they settled on one further down, just before the bend in the road. She didn't need to walk across and check. There would be a wooden gate and a path. The front door would have stained glass in it and there would be a climbing plant creeping across the brickwork.

She wouldn't go down to it, though.

She sat with her back rigid against the wooden bench and forced herself to think of other things. Her new school. She hadn't tried to make friends. There'd been no point. All around her there were the girls who stood or sat together, linking each other's arms, excluding everyone else with their giggles, their hands in front of their mouths as though that would stop anyone hearing what they were saying. She had had friends like that once; her arm had been linked and she'd heard secrets and gossip and swapped books and clothes and jewellery.

Now there was only Charlie. She'd been right about him. He had wanted her. She put her hand up to her mouth and thought about his hard fingers on her face, his hair tied so tightly at the back of his neck. In her head she pulled off the band and saw it hang over his shoulder, her fingers weaving through it.

She stopped these thoughts when a figure turned the corner.

A woman walked unsteadily, carrying two plastic carrier bags of shopping.

Lou held her breath as the woman walked slowly on the other side of the road. Her hair was short and curly, quite grey at the front. Her face was round and she was wearing glasses. She seemed to be humming something to herself and was half smiling. She had a long skirt on with a lace blouse over the top.

It was Sally, her mother, the woman in the photograph. She was sure.

Lou had imagined a huge woman with dimpled arms and a double chin. But she was only plump, not big at all.

Lou stood up as she watched the woman pause at the gate of the house she'd been avoiding looking at. The woman put the carrier bags on the ground and started to sort through a shoulder bag. She took a set of keys out and then bent over to pick her shopping up again.

Lou wanted to run over and help her.

She even took a step or two towards the edge of the road.

A car horn sounded, though, and her attention was drawn away for only a few seconds. It was Charlie, his van parked at an angle at the end of the road. She looked back towards the house in time for the door to slam. Without thinking, she walked quickly across the road and along to the house that the woman had disappeared into.

The horn sounded a couple of times but Lou stood in front of the gate. She'd been right about the creeping plant. She let her eyes rest for a few long seconds over the bright green ivy that clung fiercely to the walls of the building, curling nosily round the corners of the windows and the door.

The sound of an engine revving broke her concentration and she pulled herself away and walked slowly back to the van.

Lou was very quiet on the way home.

"You in a mood, Lulu?" Charlie said.

"Have I upset you?" he said later.

"Was I late picking you up?"

She shook her head and squeezed his arm. "I've got a bit of a headache. Too much sun, I think. I'll just close my eyes for a while and it'll go away."

She had seen her real mum.

FIFTEEN

They got back to London about nine. Charlie pulled the van up at the end of her road, a short distance away from the hostel. He switched the engine off and turned to her. She let her head move towards him until her lips parted, and then she hungrily held on to the kiss that he was giving her.

His hand was in her hair and then on her shoulder. All the while she was twisting and turning her mouth, aching with the kiss, the skin on her neck and chest tingling. Then his hand slipped on to her breast. It was only for a second, and then it was back on her shoulder. It was a brush, no more, but it sent a swoon through her.

She could have stayed in the car like that for hours, for days, for ever. Charlie slowly pulled back, though, looked at his watch and said, "I must go, Lulu."

Her eyes were still closed but she heard the rattle of his keys and the grumblings of the engine as he started the car.

"When will I see you?" she said, her voice mournful.

"I'll ring you," he said. "Or you'll probably see me at the hostel before the end of the week."

"OK," she said, sitting still. Maybe if she didn't move he would sit there for a while.

But he leaned across her and pulled on the door handle. "I really must go, Lulu," he said, and in a second she found herself out on the pavement watching the van pull away from the kerb.

"My name's Lou," she said, hugging herself with pleasure. Her hands rubbed her skin, feeling sudden goosebumps there.

Her head was full of overlapping thoughts, like a bursting suitcase that wouldn't close. Her skin was buzzing, her fingers twitching, her lips dry, chapped even, almost *weary* of the kissing.

Charlie Short: so much taller than her, so much older; someone who made her feel dizzy with anticipation, someone she could rely on.

The visit to her real mother's street sat awkwardly in the middle of these feelings, like something that had been given to her that she wasn't sure she wanted. And yet there it was: her mum's house. She had remembered it: the street, the church, the clinging ivy.

She tried to think of it with pleasure, to include it somehow in the general effervescence that had bubbled over from her day with Charlie. Instead, it gave her giant butterflies that niggled at her insides.

She turned to walk home but only took a step or two before she felt she was being watched. She stopped and looked around the street, then towards the hostel. Anna's face was at the big bay window, staring down at her.

"Mum. . ." she said, the word just jumping out before she could think, her hand rising to wave.

But Anna had turned away from the window without a wave or a smile.

Lou had never seen Anna so angry.

"You said you had a job!" she said fiercely.

"But you said you were going to a concert!" Lou said, with trepidation.

"I changed my mind. Ruth and Tommy went on their own. Never mind about me. You lied to me."

They were in the office, Lou on one side of the desk and Anna on the other. There was an invisible barrier between them and they both sat back away from it. It was like a plate-glass screen, as if it was a prison visit.

"You planned it all."

"I asked you if I could go, I did ask. If you'd said yes, I wouldn't have lied."

"So I've got to say yes to everything you want otherwise you'll lie to get your own way?"

"It was just a day out to Brighton! That was all!"

"But I'd said no. Did he know that? Did he take you out knowing I'd said no?"

"No!"

"So you lied to him as well!"

"You lie! I'm not the only one who lies!" Lou sat up, her back stiffening.

"When do I lie? I don't lie to you!"

Lou was drawing circles on the edge of the desk with her fingers. There were words that she wanted to say, statements she wanted to make, "*You stole me from my real mother. You've lied to me my whole life*," but she didn't dare. It was like a box she was afraid to open, secrets that even she couldn't mention.

"When do I lie?" Anna demanded, weaving her fingers into each other.

But Lou said nothing. Why couldn't she say it? She had the proof. She had good enough reason to fire it all back at Anna. Why didn't she do it?

Her throat began to fill up and she felt the tears behind her eyelids. She closed them and put her hands over her face.

"Oh, Lou!" Anna said, reaching her hand across the desk, breaking the partition between them. "You and me, we've always been close, we've always looked out for each other. But lately! Lately, you've changed. It's like you're a different person." Her voice was soft and she was holding Lou's hand, pulling it away from her face. Lou opened her eyes and a tear slid down her cheek.

"I'm not a different person," Lou sniffed. "It's you who has changed."

"What do you mean?" Anna sat up. "In what way?"

Lou sighed. It wasn't really what she'd wanted to say at all, but it came out anyway.

"You're always at work or with Ruth. You're always telling me to go to school. You've changed."

"So it *is* about Ruth. Is that why you lied to me? To punish me for being friends with Ruth?"

"No," she said, raising her voice, using the backs of her hands to wipe her eyes. "I wanted to go out with Charlie. I like Charlie."

"I know what it's like to want a man, but you have to be so careful. You don't know what they're like. Look at some of the women in the hostel."

"But Charlie's not like that. He's kind . . . he's gentle. . ." Anna shook her head.

"They all start like that. They're kind and gentle at the beginning. look at Ruth's husband."

"Charlie's just not like that."

"He's too old for you, Lou!"

"What about my dad?" Lou said, the words escaping before she had time to think.

Anna stiffened. She moved back, away from the edge of the table.

"What about your dad?" she said, her hands rigid, in mid-air.

"He was older than you."

A visible sigh came from her lips. Lou saw it and gritted her teeth. What had Anna expected her to say?

"A little. But I met him when I was older, not fifteen, not your age. You're not much more than a child!"

"That's it!" Lou said, her voice getting louder with each word. "When you want me to do things, leave school, move to a different part of the country, then I've got to be grown up. Then I'm to be trusted. I'm mature." As she said it her hands closed into tiny fists. "But when it's things that I want to do, then I'm only a child. Just a child. Just when it suits you!" Her voice was loud and the fists had banged down on to the table.

Anna got up and took a step backwards. She looked at Lou

with a shocked expression. After a few seconds' silence she said, "Charlie's too old for you. You're not to see him again."

"I will!" Lou stood up, her tears gone, her hands hanging down at her sides.

"You will not, Lou. These lies you've told me – it's because of him and I won't have it!"

"What right have you got to talk about lying?" Lou said it quietly, as if all her energy had gone. "You told me my dad was killed by a bomb! That was a lie. My dad never even existed. The picture from the mantelpiece was cut out of a magazine. It wasn't my dad at all. You lied. All these years you lied to me!"

Anna leant back against the filing cabinet, a look of defeat on her face. She put her knuckle into her mouth and bit on it.

"You don't know what you're talking about," she said dully. "You don't understand about your dad. I don't want to talk about it any more." Then she walked around the desk, across the office and out of the room.

Lou held her breath while the footsteps clanked down the hallway. She heard a rustle of a coat, and then the front door click open and bang closed.

Anna had gone.

Lou sat down at the table and put her hand up to her mouth as though she were gagging herself. Too late. The words had already been said.

She stayed in the office chair, unable to move, and let the room go dark around her. From different parts of the house she could hear the TV and some music, voices of the women and some babies crying.

She wondered where Anna had gone. She imagined her walking with great speed towards the flat, pacing furiously up and down the living room. She felt curiously calm, though, as if saying those hurtful things to Anna had taken some of the load from her.

It was some time later when she noticed the yellow light flashing on the telephone set. In the surrounding darkness it became a focus and she stared at it for a few moments.

It was an incoming call. Somebody was ringing for one of the women in the hostel. In a second the answer-machine would come on and record the message.

She picked the receiver up though. She would take a message. It could be important.

"Hello," she said and pronounced the number clearly and slowly. The yellow light had stopped flashing. It was still and bright and she found herself looking at it.

"Ruth Judd, please."

"She's not here at the moment," Lou said, leaning across to click on the desk lamp. She looked at her watch. It was ten-fifteen.

"Can you give her a message?" The voice was friendly, polite. After the row with Anna it was a relief to talk to anyone.

"Yes, of course. I've got a pen."

"Tell her Jack'll be seeing her sooner than she expected."

Then there was a click in her ear and the phone went dead.

Lou looked at the receiver with a sense of creeping dread. Jack was the name of Ruth's husband. She had forgotten about the code names! She had given out the information that Ruth lived here in this house to a man who was looking for her, had a history of violence against her.

She felt weak as though all her strength had gone, and lay back in the swivel chair, twisting it a little as she put her weight on it. She should go and tell Anna, maybe even ring the police. But how could she? After all that had happened?

Wouldn't it look as if she had done it on purpose?

She replaced the phone and tidied the top of the desk. In her hand was the phone log book. On the cover were the words, *ALL MESSAGES TO BE WRITTEN DOWN CLEARLY WITH THE TIME AND THE DATE.* It was heavily underlined and Lou recognized Anna's block capital letters.

Tell her Jack'll be seeing her sooner than she expected. The voice had changed then, become cold and hard, like the message she had heard on Ruth's answerphone.

The message that she had never told Anna and Ruth about.

She looked guiltily at the door. She picked up a pen and saw that her hand was shaking. She couldn't write the message down. She couldn't tell anyone. It would mean admitting that she'd messed up, forgotten about the code names. Anna might think that she had meant to do it.

She picked up other books and files that were on the desk and put them into a neat pile. Then she clicked off the desk light and, like a criminal, crept out of the room.

SIXTEEN

If only Charlie were at home. That was what Lou hoped.

By the time she found his street it was ten-thirty. She was still in the flimsy dress that she'd worn to the seaside and her arms and legs were cold. She rubbed her skin up and down and looked along the rows of houses for his number.

A young man answered the door. He had headphones on and was holding a can of lager.

"Is Charlie there?" She said it loudly, but the young man looked puzzled, pulled one ear of the headphones away and said, "What?"

"Is Charlie there?"

"Nope. The George and Dragon I should think, along the High Road."

It only took her a few minutes to walk to the pub. As she got closer she tried to imagine what it would be like. She'd decided to tell it all to Charlie and see what he'd say. It was true what Anna had said: he was older, she could confide in him. She could tell him everything and he might say, *"So what? Forget it. Anna's your mum. She's the one who brought you up!"*

This gave Lou a good feeling. If Charlie could just say that to her it would all be over. None of it would matter.

Because Anna *had* been her mother for all these years,

had loved her, cared for her. What did it matter how it had started?

But what about Sally, the woman who had had her baby snatched away?

Lou tried to imagine what Charlie would say here. "*Look, Lulu, that was all years ago. What possible good could it do to open it all up again?*"

She thought about the phone call. Charlie would tell her to go straight home and tell Anna. It was the right thing to do, she hardly needed to be told.

She hurried her steps. There was a feeling of excitement inside her. She turned the corner and saw the pub. She had a moment's loss of confidence. She'd never been inside a pub before. She was technically under age. She had no money with her to buy a drink.

She shook the worries off. Most people thought she looked older than her age. Charlie would be in the pub, he could buy her a drink. She walked up the steps of the building when something awful occurred to her. What if Charlie didn't say any of the things she wanted him to say?

She pushed open the swing doors of the pub and went inside. The smoke and noise hit her and she thought, *What if he tells me to go to the police?* To report Anna? The soles of her shoes seemed stuck to the floor and she was hemmed in on all sides by drinkers. Everyone seemed taller than her, shouting across to each other above the music on the loudspeakers. Her feet suddenly felt like lead and she inhaled a mouthful of acrid smoke from someone's cigarette.

What if Charlie were to say, "*She's committed a crime, Lou. She'll have to go to prison.*"?

She elbowed her way through and saw him across the bar, over in the far corner. She caught a glimpse of his face through a crowd of men and women holding bottles of beer and cigarettes and talking into each other's ears.

She squeezed this way and that to get past groups of young people huddled together, talking and laughing, one or two jostling about as though in a mock fight.

She saw the side of his head across someone's shoulder, and ducking and walking around another group she saw his arm along the back of a seat. She was only a metre away from where he was but she couldn't call out or even see him properly because of the crowd and the noise.

Finally she got past a group of girls who were joining in with the chorus of the song that was being played when she came in sight of him.

She had her back to the wall and was able to look over the shoulders of a couple of lads who were in front of her.

She saw Charlie, in the middle of a group of people, sitting on a bench that had a table full of glasses in front of it. At least, she saw the side of his head. His expression was one of concentration, his eyes were closed, his mouth was pushed hard on to that of a girl who was on the seat beside him.

An invisible hand seemed to twist and tug at Lou's insides and she steadied herself by feeling the wall, hard and solid, behind her.

She remembered afterwards that the girl had long fair

hair pulled up into a high ponytail on the back of her head. She remembered long sparkly earrings and hands with bright red nails holding on to Charlie's arm.

Charlie's hair was no longer tied down at the back of his neck but flowed over his shoulder, thick and smooth to the line of the ponytail, where it looked as if it had been curled and waved.

At the time, though, she only saw them together, as if they were one creature joined at the mouth. She sank back into the wall, behind the heads of the people between them, and watched as Charlie's fingers ran in and out of the girl's hair, his head moving from side to side in the kiss.

There was a pain in her chest. It felt as though a single pin had been inserted. It had gone coldly into her and out the other side. She couldn't move.

The kiss stopped and Charlie sat back on the seat, one hand pushing his hair back from his face, the other reaching across for his beer. Looking up he seemed to catch her eye. Lou held his glance for a second and then he looked away. Had he seen her? She didn't know.

She crumpled against the wall and turning, crept away, past the noise and the smoke and out of the pub.

When Lou got home the hall light was still on. She felt dazed and unable to think straight. The phone call. She would tell Anna about the phone call from Ruth's husband. She tiptoed into the living room and saw Tommy asleep on the sofa. His mouth was open and his comfort blanket was about to fall off on to the floor.

Lou squatted down and picked it up. She put it back close to Tommy's face. She also lifted a cloth monkey that had fallen and placed it at the bottom of the sofa.

She stood up and looked around, her eye settling on the empty spot on the mantelpiece where her dad's photo had been. It looked even starker than before. Looking over on the table Lou saw the packet of cigarettes, the cellophane discarded and crumpled, the cigarettes standing up out of the packet. Beside them was an ashtray and a box of matches.

She looked at it for a few moments, then walked quietly to Anna's bedroom. She opened the door so that some of the light from the hall spilled into the dark room.

Anna was in bed, under the cover. Beside her, on top of the cover, was Ruth, her uppermost arm over the top of her mum. Ruth only had her silk nightie on and her arm looked brown against Anna's white skin.

They're lying in spoons, Lou thought bitterly, *in spoons*. She pulled the door to and leant against the wall.

Let's lie in spoons, Mum. Go on, I won't fidget, I promise. Please, Mum, you be the big spoon and I'll be the little one. . .

Then she turned away and went to her room.

Why should she tell them about the phone call?

At six-thirty the next morning she walked silently down the hall towards the kitchen. In her hand she had a notepad, on which she'd written:

I'm going away for a while. I've had to take some money. Don't look for me. Lou.

She had a small holdall with some clothes and toiletries in it. Over it was her jacket. She picked up Anna's handbag and took her purse from it.

There were two twenty-pound notes. She took one. All she needed was her fare down to Shoreham. It wasn't stealing, not really, not like Anna had done.

When she got to Shoreham her *real mum* would look after her.

PART THREE

SEVENTEEN

There was no direct train to Shoreham. She had to change and wait around in the cold morning sun. When she arrived it was just past eight o'clock.

All the way down in the train she rehearsed what she was going to say.

"I'm your daughter who was stolen from you. The woman who stole me loved me and cared for me. That's why I can't tell you who she is. But I've come back now to my real family."

No one would ever know that Anna was the person who took her away.

She made herself think about the first meeting over and over again.

It stopped her thinking of the things she had left behind, the past.

When she got off the train at Shoreham it was warming up. She walked out of the station and through the shopping area. Within minutes she was alongside the sea. Even that early there were families walking along the edge, small children chasing the waves, a couple walking stiffly apart and some teenagers, pushing each other's shoulders and holding their lit cigarettes flagrantly, so that everyone could see.

Along the concrete walkway there were several single

people walking their dogs and a man pulling up the shutters on a wooden hut that said, *Beach Café, teas, ices, hot dogs.*

Lou stood for a moment, not knowing quite what to do. She looked at her watch.

Anna would be up by now and have found the note. Lou felt a mild nausea in her stomach. She put the palm of her hand on her rib cage. It was because she hadn't eaten. It was nothing to do with her image of Anna, the piece of paper trembling in her hand, her purse lying open with only one twenty-pound note in it instead of two.

She had stolen from Anna.

Her throat constricted. She saw a look of physical pain on Anna's face, as if she had struck her in some way. She imagined Anna's shock at seeing the money gone, Lou's clothes not in her chest of drawers, the overnight bag missing. Anna would be walking up and down the living room, one cigarette after another in her mouth. Ruth would be trying to calm the situation; Lou visualized her black hair wild and electric after having just woken up. Tommy would probably be by Ruth, unsure of what was happening. He might say, "*Where's Lou? Where's Lou?*" and when no one answered him he'd sit on the sofa with his blanket, his thumb creeping up to his mouth, his tiny glasses smeared and needing a good clean.

Lou's legs felt weak; it was as if her bones had become soft and slack, and would only hold her up for a few more seconds. She moved towards the beach wall and sat on it.

What had she done?

She wanted to be with Anna, to link her arm, to hug her neck, to snuggle in beside her under her duvet. But Anna was not her real mother.

And what about Ruth's husband? Was he on his way, at that moment, to the hostel? She looked around and a phone box caught her eye. She could ring her, just say that she was all right, that Anna needn't worry about her any more. She could promise to repay the twenty pounds when she got settled. She could tell her about the phone call.

But she couldn't.

The sound of Anna's voice would make her want to go home again. Anna was part of the past that she was moving away from. She needed to forget about it all, to think about other things.

She got up and began to walk back towards the shops. It was almost ten o'clock. How early could she go and see Sally? Explain it to her? Perhaps she could use Sally's phone to contact the hostel anonymously, to let them know that Ruth's husband was on his way?

She stood by the side of the road in complete confusion. What had she come here for? What had she thought she could achieve?

A bus whooshed past her at that moment. It pulled into the pavement about twenty metres ahead. On the back were the words, *South Coast Road Express, Brighton.* She looked around hopelessly. She just needed time to think. After only a moment's hesitation she started to run towards the bus.

Brighton was just waking up. The shopkeepers were stacking up their sticks of rock, setting piles of funny hats and colourful beach balls out on to the pavements in front of their shops. Lou stood for a few seconds after the bus had dropped her off and looked up and down the road. In the distance she could see the pier where she and Charlie had walked. It had only been twenty-four hours before but it felt like a lifetime.

She found herself squinting into the sun and searched in her bag for the sunglasses that Charlie had bought for her. She couldn't find them, though, and squatted down on the pavement to see if they were in her overnight bag. Her eye settled on a couple who were leaning lazily against a wall across the street. They were young, about Lou's age. The girl had her back to the wall and the boy was facing her, his arms on her shoulders, kissing her lightly on the mouth.

She deliberately looked away, her fingers touching the plastic glasses, pulling them out of the bag and putting them on.

As she stood up, a man knocked into her saying, "*Sorry, luv.*" He was being pulled along by a dog on a lead. Lou saw that his hair was long and he had it tied at the neck into a ponytail. She closed her eyes and walked on, in the direction of the pier. She could see it stretching far out into the sea. In the distance she thought she could see some of the fishermen, leaning on the rails, their rods invisible to her eye. She remembered some of them turning round to look at her and Charlie when they'd been kissing.

Charlie.

She could almost hear the noise of the pub and smell the sourness of the beer and smoke. She could even remember the heat of all the bodies crowded into the bar, she pushing by, saying *"Excuse me, please. Sorry, can I just get past? Could I just squeeze through?"* Having to shout to be heard above the music from the speakers.

She shook her head and turned on to the pier. Underneath her feet she focused on the thick wooden boards that divided her from the sea; in between the cracks she could see the dark water, frothy at the edges, slurping around beneath her.

The kiss.

She had a snapshot in her head. The two of them, Charlie and the girl, his hair hanging over his shoulder, hers up in a high ponytail, her earring dangling, their faces at angles so that their mouths fitted.

Lou could almost *feel* the kiss herself.

But the rawness in her throat broke her reverie. She tried to swallow but her mouth was dry and empty.

Suddenly she couldn't walk any further along the pier, couldn't face the squawks of the seagulls or the smell of the sea or the feel of the soft moving boards under her feet.

Charlie and Lou.

What a fool she had been.

*

Some hours later she found herself wandering down the tiny Lanes that crisscrossed the back streets of Brighton, the sea far away, out of sight. In no time at all she was standing in front of *Master Simon's Antiques*.

The rocking horse was still there, its eyes glittering like precious stones, its upholstery looking smarter than she remembered. Had she ever ridden on it? She tried hard to think back, to put the little girl in the sailor dress on to the back of the giant toy, to feel the rocking, to and fro, the little girl's head going up and down, up and down.

But no memory came and she stood foolishly in the middle of a strange place where she knew no one and no one knew her. She turned, not quite knowing what to do, and found herself going through the smoked-glass door, hearing the "ting" as she entered the dark, shadowy shop.

A woman was down the far end, behind an old desk. She looked up briefly, then went back to her papers. Lou was surrounded by chests of drawers and shiny brown shelving, lampstands with fringes hanging off them, pictures on the wall with gilt frames, views of country mansions, men in doublets standing with a gun in one hand and dogs around their feet. There was china everywhere: giant soup tureens with edges as fine as lace, tiny cups and saucers, their handles so fragile that a cross word could have broken them.

"Can I help you?" the woman called from the other end of the shop.

"Yes, no." Lou didn't know what to say or why she had come inside. She turned to look at the wall to her left and saw that it was covered in newspaper articles, framed in glass. The Outbreak of the Second World War; Votes for Women; The Sinking of the Titanic; The Assassination of President Kennedy. Lou let her eye scan over them until she came to one at the bottom right-hand corner. It was newer than the rest and didn't really seem to fit in. As she read it she could hear the woman's heels clicking across the floor. *Child Snatched from Pushchair*, she read.

"That always causes interest." Lou heard the woman's voice as she came up to her.

"What happened?" Lou found herself saying.

"Oh, dreadful it was. Along the coast, in Shoreham. My brother, who owned this shop, God rest his soul, he knew the mother, Sally Robinson. He was quite friendly with her. It was awful. It was the talk of the town. In a pushchair she was. The mother just left her for a couple of minutes and she was gone. They found her shoe on the clifftop path. The whole of Shoreham turned out. Loads of people from Brighton, too. My brother as well. Hundreds of people walking across the cliffs, looking for her. They found a rattle and pair of gloves. That was all."

Lou pictured it: a line of people that stretched for ever, walking across the cliffs, hand in hand, looking for the missing child. Maybe Sally went there as well, walking, her eyes searching for any clue. Maybe, when they found nothing, she went and stood by the edge of the cliff, looking over at the rocks below.

"My brother, God rest his soul, was very upset by it."

The sound of a "ting" made Lou jump as the door

135

opened behind her and three people came in, laughing with each other, the tail end of their conversation spilling into the shop.

The woman backed away from Lou and immediately smiled at them. They were middle-aged, expensively dressed, one had a camera case draped over his arm.

"Can I help you?" The woman's voice rose at the end, full of expectation.

Lou took a last look at the newspaper on the wall and quietly excused herself from the shop.

Back in Shoreham Lou bought some chips and sat on the sea wall again. It was almost six o'clock. She'd been full of plans when she'd left London that morning but she'd spent the whole day being aimless.

The chips were hot and she had to hold each one in her fingers for a moment before she put it into her mouth. They had found a rattle and a pair of gloves along the cliff. Somebody in the long line of people had spotted them, picked them up, flushed with excitement, rushed across to the nearest police officer. Maybe the word had spread along the line, "*They've found something, someone's found some gloves and a toy, some clothes have been found, the girl's clothes have been found.*" Had anybody misheard it? Hearing what they had wanted to hear? "*They've found the girl!*" A sense of relief like intoxication spreading through the line?

But the girl hadn't been found. She'd been whisked away, was sitting in a room somewhere with Anna.

Lou got up and began to walk again, her overnight bag on one shoulder and then on the other. She stopped and leant on walls or sat on benches. She bought two ice-cold cans of fizzy drink and a chocolate bar. She walked along the shingle, looking up from time to time at the cliffs, jutting out like a cold shoulder. Then she walked back.

Occasionally she passed a phone box that seemed to call out to her.

She could go back to Anna as if none of it had ever happened.

It wasn't too late.

It was seven o'clock when she knocked on the door of the house in Swallow Drive. It opened almost immediately.

Sally Robinson stood there in front of her, as if she'd been only centimetres behind the door, waiting to open it. She was wearing a loose floral dress and Lou reached out her hand, not quite sure what to say or do.

"Oh, Lou. Thank God you're here," Sally said, gripping her arm with unexpected strength.

"I . . . I. . ." All the words Lou had rehearsed slipped and she was speechless.

"We've been waiting for you. Where on earth have you been?" Sally said, and Lou found herself startled by the greeting. Was it possible that after all these years Sally was sitting, waiting for every knock at the door, expecting her grown-up daughter to be on the other side?

"George, she's here. Quick, George. Lou's arrived!"

"I've been walking around. . ." was all Lou could say.

Could her real mother recognize her so suddenly? Know her instantly after twelve or more years?

A man came up the hall behind Sally and peeped over her shoulder. He was thin and old, not at all like Lou had imagined her dad to be. She felt a stab of disappointment. He squeezed past his wife and came forward.

"We've been worried sick, Lou. Where have you been?" he said.

"I've been . . . I've been. . ." But Lou couldn't say any more. She couldn't tell them where she'd been all of those years.

"Don't keep the girl out in the street!" Sally said, and pushed past him so that she was now on the porch beside Lou. "Come in, Lou, come on in."

Lou allowed herself to be led into the house. Questions raced about in her head. Had they expected her? Could they know their own daughter so instantly?

"We've been waiting for you, haven't we, George?"

"What've you been doing?" George said, patting her on the shoulder. His hair was wispy across his scalp and his hand was so thin that she could see the veins protruding. She looked at Sally's dress, big and shapeless, her plump arm spilling out of it. This was her real mum and dad, and yet she had never felt so strange, so out of place.

"She looks tired out!" Sally said, a bright smile on her face.

How could they be like this? Lou had expected tears, hugs, surprise, amazement. She had even thought they might not believe her, possibly be hostile towards her. After all, what proof did she have? Instead she had been greeted like an expected guest.

She found herself being gently directed into a tiny living room with a big bay window. She felt curiously deflated and walked across to it, no longer hearing all of Sally's words. She'd done the wrong thing in coming here, she was sure. She looked out through the glass and could see the church across the way and some small children playing by the wall with a toy pram and some dolls. Out of the corner of her eye she noticed a taxi cab coming down the street and pulling up along the way.

"You'll be wanting to meet our Louise," Sally said, her smile bright and reassuring. Lou could hear footsteps on the stairs. Somebody was coming who Sally wanted her to meet. A glance round at the window and Lou could see the taxi pulling up a few metres away from the house. A taxi. An idea took hold of her. It would only take a second for her to walk past her real mum, past her real dad, and get into that taxi and go back to London to be with Anna. With absolute certainty she knew that was what she wanted to do. She even felt herself take a step in the direction of the door, only to be stopped by the appearance of a young girl of about thirteen.

"Hi," the girl said, an embarrassed look on her face, "I'm Louise."

The girl was wearing denim shorts and a T-shirt. She was short and plump, like Sally. She had her hair up in an off-centre ponytail. She was smiling, looking at Sally slyly, as though they were sharing a secret together. Lou's forehead creased and she looked hard at the girl.

"This is Louise," Sally said, as if it were important that she confirmed the girl's information.

In the back of her head Lou heard a car door slam. In a few moments the taxi would be gone and she would have lost her chance to get away and back to London.

"Louise is our daughter," Sally was saying. "This Louise is *our* daughter," but Lou wasn't listening. She had made her decision.

"I'm sorry, I have to go," she said, and passed her real mum – heading for the taxi that had just dropped someone off and would be leaving any minute. In the hallway her real dad was standing looking worried and she walked past him with a feeling of guilt for what she was about to do.

The front door pulled open easily and she turned round to say something to them, some kind of goodbye, some sort of explanation. Something stopped her. Out of the corner of her eye she glimpsed a familiar face, her mouth falling open with shock.

It was Anna, paying the taxi driver. Anna her mum, looking flustered, turning towards her with a look of frozen anguish on her face.

"Lou!" she said, and shoved her money at the driver.

"Mum!" Lou said, her heart suddenly as light as a balloon.

In three steps Anna was hugging her, her arms tightly around Lou's back, her head buried deep into Lou's shoulder, her voice muffled.

"Oh my God! Lou, I thought I'd lost you! I thought I'd lost you," she said and Lou held her tight, looking round at Sally Robinson, her husband George and their daughter Louise.

After a few seconds she said, "I don't understand."

EIGHTEEN

Lou and Anna were sitting on a sofa in the tiny living room. Lou could still see out of the window to where the children were playing with their toys. The church behind them was in shadow and looked dark and mysterious. The taxi had gone some time before.

In front of them was a coffee table. On it Anna had laid out the contents of Lou's package of evidence: the letter from Sally, the photograph of the little girl in the sailor dress, the newspaper cutting about the disappearance of Sally's child.

"I found these first thing this morning, when I looked through your drawers, after I got your note. I knew you'd been acting strangely lately. I can't understand why you didn't come and ask me about all this as soon as you'd found them."

Lou said nothing. They were on their own. She could hear Sally and George from the kitchen, their voices low, the sound of the cups and saucers. Sally's daughter, Louise, had gone back upstairs. Lou could hear music playing from above.

"Was it because I've become so close to Ruth?"

Why did she always refer to that? As if Lou cared.

"What about my dad?" she finally said. "You lied to me about my dad."

"I did. And it's something I've always regretted but never known how to get out of. It's the little lie you tell one day that grows and grows until it's so big, so important that it's impossible to put it right."

"You let me believe, all these years, that he was killed by a bomb."

Anna shook her head. "It was never that calculated. You asked me once what your dad was and I told you he was a soldier. That was true. Then you said, one day, was he killed in a war? The way children do. You had an imagination. You'd probably seen a film or something. So I said yes, sort of. Then you wanted to know where, when, why and all the rest. As you got older you wouldn't be fobbed off with vague answers. I had to be precise. So the lie grew and grew until I almost began to believe it myself."

The door opened and Sally came in with a tray.

"Lou, fancy you thinking you were my daughter!"

Lou smiled weakly.

"And you remembering the day at Brighton. My, you were only two. You couldn't have been more than two! That was a lovely day. It wasn't long after that your mum came and took you back. My, I missed you when you went! Remember how I cried, Jill?"

Anna smiled. Jill Peterson was her real name.

"I still don't understand," Lou said, nodding her head when George offered her a biscuit, the plate trembling in his bony hand.

"Let's start at the beginning, then," Sally said, sitting

down on an armchair, moving from side to side, making herself comfortable. She furrowed her eyebrows for a moment and looked in deep concentration. "Your mum was working in a job in the Midlands and wanted me to look after you while she got settled."

"I needed to get enough money together. I needed to do the job right. A baby would have made it difficult, so Sally. . ."

"Your mum and me knew each other from school. We were great friends!"

"Sally looked after you for about a year. I came to see you as often as I could."

"You did, Jill."

"I missed you terribly, but I had good reasons why I needed to be on my own."

"We got on great, you and me, Lou. Great friends we were. But I knew you were Jill's baby and that one day you'd go home."

"That's why we had our own," George spoke.

"That's right. While you were here I got pregnant. When Jill finally came for you I was only weeks away from having my own baby. A little girl she was."

"But. . ." Lou said.

"And I called her Lou, after you. I thought I'd probably never see you again, so I called her Louise."

"And she was stolen away."

"Yes, she was," Sally said, smoothing down her skirt. "For five days she was missing. The whole village was out searching for her. It was on nationwide telly and we thought . . . well, we thought the worst, didn't we, George?"

"We did indeed." George reached over and took Sally's hand.

"Then we got a phone call from the vicar of the church across the road. We rushed across there, didn't we? And there she was, in her pushchair, smiling, well dressed, well washed, well fed, with no visible signs of any harm. She had a complete set of new clothes."

"And more in a bag," George said.

"My! We were so pleased to see her." Sally stopped for a minute, staring into space. From upstairs Lou could still hear the thudding of pop music.

"There was a letter," George said.

"Yes, a letter. I've still got it. The police gave it to me when they closed the case." Sally got up and went across to a drawer.

"Here," she handed the letter to Lou. "You never saw this, did you, Jill?"

"No," Anna said.

The letter had yellowed over the years. It was on lined paper, the writing spidery and faint. Lou read it out loud.

"*Dear parent. Here is your baby. I'm desperately sorry I took her but I lost my own little girl two months ago. I've taken good care of her and treated her well. More than anything I'd like to keep her but it's not right. Please forgive me.*"

She handed it to Anna.

"Did they find the woman?"

"Yes. Some weeks after. They went to the local hospitals and found the names of people who had lost children a couple of months before. They got doctors and health visitors to do the enquiries. They finally came up with a woman who lived in Brighton."

"Did you ever meet her?"

"No, I couldn't do that. I felt sorry for the woman but I couldn't forgive her for taking my Lou away."

Sally was shaking her head as the phone began to ring. George got up from his seat to answer it.

"Does your daughter remember any of it?"

"Good Lord no! She was hardly a year old. It doesn't seem to have affected her at all. Except of course that she became famous!"

"What's she like, your Louise?" Anna said.

"She's lovely. Different from this Lou. She slept at night. Your daughter never did!"

George came into the room. "It's for you, Jill," he said. "Someone called Ruth."

"Oh!" Anna looked flustered. "I won't be a second."

Lou held her breath. *Ruth's husband. Was that what the phone call was about?*

"That your mum's friend?" Sally said, looking over the top of her teacup at George.

"One thing I don't understand," Lou said, her mum's voice barely audible from the hallway. "Why exactly did my mum leave me here and go to work in the Midlands? Why not leave me closer, somewhere nearby? And why did she change her name?"

Sally opened her mouth to speak and looked at George again.

Lou heard the "ting" of the phone and Anna came back into the room.

"Sal, I'm sorry, we'll have to go. That was my friend Ruth. Somehow her ex-husband has got hold of her address. He rang the hostel this afternoon and said he was coming to see her. She's terribly upset."

"Has she rung the police?" Lou said. She had a sudden memory of his voice on Ruth's answerphone: *Ruth, there's no point in hiding. I'll find you in the end.*

"Yes. They say they'll cruise around but Ruth's in a terrible state. We'll have to go, Sally. I'm sorry. I had hoped to spend some time here."

"OK, Jill, love. We'll take you to Brighton station. There's a direct train to London from there."

"Oh, would you, George? Thanks." Anna was banging her knuckles together. She turned to Lou. "Will you come home with me, Lou? I really need you now. All the other things we can sort out."

Lou nodded, a leaden feeling in her chest. Everything had happened so quickly. She just hadn't had time to tell her mum about the phone call. How could she tell her now?

They were in Brighton in minutes. George and Sally got out of the car while they bought the tickets. There was hugging and kissing on the platform.

"Don't leave it so long next time to come and see us," Sally said, her dress billowing up in the breeze.

"Ten years or more!" George said. He'd put a suit jacket on and looked as if he was on his way to a wedding.

"You know why!" Anna said, giving each of them a hug.

As the train moved away, Lou looked at Sally and George. A big plump lady with a small skinny man. They looked like a couple from a seaside postcard. She was secretly glad that they weren't her mum and dad. She linked arms with Anna and waved at the couple on the platform.

All the way to London she held fiercely on to Anna's arm. She had almost lost her. She tried not to think about Ruth's husband and the phone call. No one could know that she had given the game away, that she was responsible. No one could know.

Only she would know.

Lou sat quietly and thought about it all the way to London.

NINETEEN

It was dark by the time they got back. The hostel looked tranquil and the street looked quiet. They got out of the taxi and quickly paid the driver. The windows were intact and there was no sign of any disturbance. Lou and Anna walked quickly up the steps and in the front door. Once inside, they went into the office. Ruth was there, standing by the desk. Tommy was sitting in an armchair. Standing at the window was a WPC, talking softly into her radio. The sounds from the rest of the house were normal: music playing, the TV from the lounge, running water from the bathroom, voices of small children playing games.

Lou let her breath out. There had been no damage. Ruth seemed calm. Tommy smiled at her when she came in although he didn't get out of his chair to run towards her. She noticed his blanket wrapped around his arm and pushed against the side of his face.

"Is everything all right?" Anna said, walking across to Ruth.

Lou watched as Anna and Ruth hugged each other. Ruth buried her face into Anna's shoulder and Anna stroked Ruth's hair over and over, while saying, "It's all right, it's all right." They looked like long-lost lovers.

"I'll have to move," Ruth said. Her voice sounded wet with sobs.

"No, you won't."

"You don't know what he's like," she said.

The WPC watched impassively. Lou felt embarrassed and turned away to look out of the window. Something was happening between her mum and Ruth. She couldn't put a name to it, wasn't sure what it was. A car passed by, its headlights illuminating the street for a moment.

"I'll be on my way," the WPC said, "now that you're back, Miss Lewis."

"Can't you stay?" Anna said.

"Not really. I've been here for hours. If he turns up at all, just ring the station. There'll be a car here in minutes."

Anna walked out to the front door with the WPC. Lou could hear them talking.

"He won't come," the WPC said. "He knows that the conditions of the Court Order forbid him to be within half a mile of his wife. He'll face a prison sentence if he comes."

"I hope you're right," Anna said.

"I'm sure I am. Some of them just like to threaten, to make the woman feel afraid. That's a big enough victory for them. He won't come. He's probably miles away."

He came about an hour later.

Ruth and Tommy had gone up to bed. Anna and Lou had got sleeping bags out of the store and were going to bed down on the floor of the office. Anna was in the middle of a phone call to the duty social worker, discussing another placement for Ruth. Lou was lying, zipped up on the floor, thinking about the events of the day.

Suddenly Anna's voice was louder.

"Hello? Hello?" she said, and shook the phone receiver, crossly. "I've been cut off." She punched the buttons on the set again.

"What's the matter?" Lou said.

"There's no sound. How odd."

Lou unzipped her sleeping bag and got up. Anna was pressing all the buttons on the machine, growing increasingly annoyed.

"What on earth?" she said and then stopped, holding the receiver in mid-air, her face clearing.

"We've been cut off," she said. "Someone's cut us off!"

Anna got up and walked across to the window. She looked out of the side of the blind.

"He's cut the phone line. Ruth's husband has cut the phone line."

Lou couldn't speak. A mixture of fright and guilt stopped her saying anything. It was going to be bad after all. He was going to come and make trouble, and it was all her fault. She had given him the information that Ruth was here and now they couldn't even call for help.

A slow knock at the front door jolted her out of it.

"It's him," Anna said. She turned to Lou. "Stay here, don't come out into the hall."

"It's my fault," Lou said, tears coming out of her eyes. "I told him she was here. I didn't mean to – it was an accident."

But Anna had left the room and gone into the hall. Lou followed her, her feet dragging behind.

The banging on the front door was slow, unhurried, calm.

Anna put the chain on and pulled the door back a few inches. Lou watched her. A couple of the women from the downstairs rooms came out into the hall.

"I wish to speak to my wife, Ruth Judd," a voice said.

"I'm afraid she's not here any more. She was moved on this afternoon."

"I know she's there." The voice was low, calm.

"You're mistaken. She moved on today. In any case, we don't allow any visitors after seven."

"Just tell Ruth I'd like to speak to her." The voice was insistent but polite. Quite unlike the cold, hard voice that Lou had heard over the phone.

"She's not here. I'll have to call the police if you don't go."

"Come now, Miss Lewis. You won't be able to. I believe your phones are out of order." He said it like a British Telecom operator. *I'm sorry, caller, I'm afraid the lines are out of order.*

More of the women had come out of their rooms, out of the TV lounge and along the hallway. Some of them were in dressing gowns, others still in their jeans or leggings. Up at the top of the stairs Lou could see Ruth's frightened face, her black hair, unruly, standing out from her head.

"I'm closing this door now," Anna said, her voice level.

His fist came through the glass without any warning.

Lou saw it in slow motion. First there was the leaded glass, red and blue and yellow, a mosaic pattern. A moment's silence that was heavy, weighted. Then a punching sound and the shattering of glass. The coloured shards scattering like shrapnel across the hall floor.

Anna jumped back as the man's hand came through and unhooked the safety chain. It only took a few seconds and the front door was swinging open.

Some of the women gave a gasp and there was a shuffling of people moving back away from the door. Many were quiet though, their silence like a wall around them. Lou felt them harden their shoulders, the skin on their arms like tough leather.

Anna was in the middle and took a step forward, in front of the women and closer to the man. Lou opened her mouth to tell her not to but no words came out. The man was facing them.

Ruth's husband, Mr Judd. He was taller than Anna and his hair was receding. He had a mac on, pale and long, past his knees. Lou was reminded, for a moment, of the man who had chased them at the funfair two years before. He looked completely different, though, not dark and mysterious but everyday, ordinary, like a salesman in a shop.

"If you let me speak to Ruth I'll be on my way. That's not much to ask, is it? Just a few minutes with my wife. Then no one will get hurt." He was rubbing his hand, the one that had come through the glass. Lou noticed a bubble of blood near his knuckle.

"Anna." Ruth's voice sounded from behind, up the stairs. There were about fifteen women between her and her husband.

"Stay where you are, Ruth," Anna said steadily.

"She wants to talk to me. Why are you stopping her, young lady?" There was an edge to the man's voice and Lou watched as a line of blood dripped from his fist on to his cream mac.

"I insist that you leave!" Anna raised her voice like a school teacher's.

The man smiled, almost sadly, and then without warning his other arm hit out at the wall and sent a picture flying off, missing Anna by centimetres and slamming against the banister.

There was a collective gasp and all the women came closer to Anna, huddling around her. They made a cordon across the hallway and stairs, about twenty of them by then. Somewhere at the back was Ruth, looking on like a frightened animal.

"I insist that you let me speak to my wife," he said, and looked at his damaged hand, down which ran rivulets of blood.

The women seemed to move closer together, though, and Lou could feel shoulders tightly up against hers, hot breath on the back of her neck. They didn't seem like individual women any more; they were together, a body of women, blocking the hallway.

Opposite them the man looked confused, distracted, glancing now and then at his bloody hand. He took a step backwards against the door, his feet crunching some of the broken glass. He seemed visibly to shrink in size. He clearly didn't know what to do. His eyes darted from one side to the other and up to the top of the stairs where his wife was. His breathing was quick and he looked back at the door that he had broken and then to the picture that lay on the floor. His hand was crimson and Lou couldn't take her eyes off it.

Then, without a word, he abruptly turned and left, leaving the front door open.

They stayed standing closely together for some seconds after his back had disappeared down the stairs and turned away from the house.

Anna was the first to speak.

"You three," she turned to the women directly behind her. "Go next door and use their phone. Get the police here."

Then she closed the door, gingerly stepping over the broken glass that was lying on the floor. The group of women seemed to fall apart in a moment, some laughing exaggeratedly, some saying nothing, just sitting back on the stairs or walking off to their own room. One or two looked visibly shaken, their eyes glassy and their lips glued together.

Lou closed her eyes. *It had all been her fault.*

In the office a different WPC was sitting in the armchair having a cup of tea. Ruth was talking quietly to her. Tommy was on Ruth's knee.

"I'm sorry, Mum." Lou said it for the tenth time.

"I know you are. It's not your fault. He was so determined he would have found her in the end. Sometimes you have to stop running away."

As she and Anna left the hostel Arthur was driving up. Lou could see Charlie in the van beside him.

"Annie," Arthur said, "not again. What are these blokes thinking of? Lock them up and throw away the key! That's what I say."

Charlie was carrying an oblong piece of wood. He came up to her as she was at the gate.

"Hi, Lou. You all right? You didn't get hurt?"

"No, I'm fine," she said.

"Did you come round to see me at the flat last night?"

She looked up at his face, his hair tied back. She remembered his kisses and his hands on her skin, his whispered voice in her ear.

"No," she said. "It must have been one of your other girlfriends." She laughed, even though she didn't feel like it.

"Now, Lulu," Charlie said, relief in his voice, "you know you're my only love."

"Yes, I know," she said, and walked off up the road after Anna.

TWENTY

On the table, in front of Lou, Anna had placed a box. It was the size of a shoebox and the corners of it had been reinforced with Sellotape over the years.

"I want you to look at these things while I make a cup of tea. Then I'll try to explain it all to you."

Lou unpacked the box slowly, as though it were full of fragile things: delicate china, glass ornaments, objects that she might break if she handled them too harshly.

In fact, it was full of bits of paper and photographs. The top piece that she came across was her own birth certificate. She looked it over. *Louise Peterson. Father: Robert Peterson. Mother: Jill Peterson. Place of birth: Kirkby District Hospital, Buckinghamshire.*

She had been born in Buckinghamshire.

Underneath, there were several photographs. A man in an army uniform holding a tiny baby on his lap. The same day but a few minutes later when the man was holding the tiny baby up in the air, looking lovingly at her. A wedding photo: the same man in a dark suit and Anna, much younger, a foolish grin on her face, a white dress and veil filling all the space in the photograph.

There were several more like that, one with some people surrounding the couple, confetti in the air, flowers and smiles in abundance. Other photographs had been taken in the garden of a house. In the background was a blow-up paddling pool and the man was in shorts, holding a garden hose that was filling it. A tiny toddler was in front only wearing a pair of pants, looking quizzically at the camera.

Underneath there were letters, dozens of them. The note paper was official and had the heading *Sussex Regiment. Dear Jill*, they all started. *I love you. . . I'm missing you. . . I'm counting the days until I see you again. . . Give Lou a big kiss from me. . . Make sure that Lou is being a good girl. . . Don't let Lou forget me. . .* And so they went on, pages and pages, sometimes the handwriting becoming so slanted it was difficult to read.

Underneath it all Lou found another photograph. It was a head and shoulders pose of Robert Peterson, in his army uniform. It wasn't unlike the fake photograph in the frame that she had carried from flat to flat, from town to town. The man in it was mildly familiar, as if Lou had seen him somewhere, had come face to face with him.

Her dad.

Why had Anna kept these things from her? Why had she used a picture of a stranger when they had these photographs all this time?

Anna came through into the room carrying two mugs of tea. She looked wary, concerned.

Lou suddenly felt overwhelmed with sadness; like an invisible cloud it seemed to surround her and press down on her shoulders. Anna looked at her with sympathy, placing the mugs gently on the table and reaching out for Lou's hand.

"I don't understand," Lou said, the words croaking out. "Did my dad die in Northern Ireland or not?"

"No," Anna said. "Your dad didn't die. He's still alive and for the last thirteen years he's been trying to find us."

"But. . ." Lou said. A man in a long raincoat came into her head. The noise of the fair, the flashing lights of the carousels, the screams from the ghost train.

"We've been running away from him. I've been trying to get away from him. . ."

"But why?" Lou said, a hint of anger in her voice. She was looking at the photographs and letters that covered the table top: her dad, her family, her life that Anna had taken her away from.

"Because I knew that if I stayed with him, one day he would kill me."

They were on the settee and Anna was talking in a low voice. In her hand was the packet of cigarettes that had been on the table. Anna was holding the box, feeling the cigarettes as she spoke.

"I was much younger than him, only seventeen when we met. He was twenty-five and had been in the army since he left school. My mum died suddenly of a heart attack two days before my eighteenth birthday. After the funeral Robert asked me to marry him. There seemed no reason not to. I loved him and there was no point in waiting. That's how it seemed at the time."

Anna was quiet for a minute, as if she was trying to sort out what to say next.

"We were happy at first. It was all redecorating and trips out into the countryside. I got pregnant almost immediately. Everything seemed to be going well. When you were about nine months old he was sent to Northern Ireland. He was there for six months and he came back a different man. I don't know why. I know it must have been bad over there but he changed towards me."

"Did he miss me?" was all Lou could think of to say.

"Oh, yes. He adored you."

"How did he change? When he came back from Northern Ireland?"

"He was distant, spent hours on his own or out with his friends. He drank a lot then as well. He wouldn't talk about the tour of duty. I don't know, I never understood what it was that changed him."

Lou looked at the photo of the man in uniform that she had in her hand. The man who had chased them through the fair on that cold spring night, when she and Anna had run like blazes across the common and hidden in the dark streets. The man who would have taken her to Disneyland, her dad.

"The first time he hit me was over something very minor. A row over something that had been misplaced – lost. He was arguing one minute and the next I felt the flat of his hand hit the side of my face. He had such rage, like it all came out in an eruption. I hadn't seen it coming. I hadn't thought for a minute that he would ever do that to me. I can still remember my skin stinging for hours afterwards."

Lou pressed her lips together and kept looking at the flat photograph, the still face. *Don't let Lou forget me. . .*

"I had a purple bruise down my cheek. He said he was sorry. Blamed it on the fact that he was stressed, worried about his promotion. Blamed it on everything but himself."

"Did you leave him?" Lou said.

"No. Goodness! Not then. I stayed for months after that. I told myself it was my fault. If I understood him better, if I organized things at home more efficiently, if I loved him more, it would change. He would go back to being the man I had first met."

Anna took one of the cigarettes and put it between her lips.

"Weeks would go by when he didn't hit me and then, without warning, something would upset him. Each time it seemed to get worse. I had a broken arm and two broken ribs. I had black eyes and a scratch down my face where his ring had caught my skin. I had bruises all over my back and my chest.

"One day, when he'd gone away fishing with his friends for the weekend, I stood in front of the mirror and looked at myself. It looked like I'd been in a car accident. I hated myself."

"Oh, Mum," Lou said, holding Anna's arm tightly, looking up and down her skin to see if, even after all this time, there might be some scars left.

"I thought it was my fault, you see. I thought I was to blame." Anna picked up the box of matches and struck one. She fed the flame to the cigarette and inhaled deeply.

The smell of sulphur hung in the air after the match had been blown out.

"That weekend he came back drunk and pushed me so hard that I fell over and hit my head on the corner of the kitchen table. I was unconscious for some minutes. He told me so afterwards. But you know what was worse? Worse even than pushing me?"

Lou said nothing; the back of her throat seemed as though it was on fire.

"He didn't ring for an ambulance. He was too ashamed of what he'd done. He just hoped that I would wake up. That time I did, but I knew that one day I wouldn't. If I stayed with him, one day I would lie on that floor and I'd never get up again."

Anna inhaled on the cigarette and blew the smoke away from Lou. It seemed as though she was about to speak even though nothing came out. Eventually she said, "So I left. I waited till he was away overnight and I took what I could carry and left. I took a coach to Shoreham and left you with Sally and then went to the Midlands to find a job. I knew he'd look for us. I knew he'd be looking for a woman with a baby so I left you somewhere he'd never known about. When I got settled I went and got you from Sally. You cried when I took you away. It really was as if you thought I was stealing you from your real mum."

Lou remembered the other little girl who really had been stolen, snatched away, from outside the chemist's shop.

"I don't know if he was ever close to finding us, I'm really not sure. We never saw him again, at least. . ."

"Until the fair, two years ago," Lou interrupted.

Anna was nodding her head. "I was so stupid. It had been so long, ten, eleven years since I'd seen him, since he'd seen you. As far as he knew we could both have been dead. I began to think it wasn't fair, that you were his daughter after all and he had a right to know that you were alive, healthy, happy even."

"I was," Lou said decisively, as though Anna had just been saying the opposite.

"So I wrote to him. I sent him a photo of you. I even posted it from a box near the flat that we were living in."

"And he came looking for us?"

"Yes. When I saw him there, at the fair, I felt my legs turn to jelly and I realized that even then, even after all those years, I was still afraid of him."

"That's why we moved."

"Yes. He didn't have our address but it was only a matter of time before he would have found us."

"Oh, Mum," Lou said. "Why didn't you just tell me? Why did you make up all those lies?"

"I didn't mean to. He was your dad. Your flesh and blood. I didn't want you to know what sort of a person he was. It was easier to make the whole thing into a kind of story."

"But did you think I was going to be like him?" Lou felt her teeth grind together.

"What do you mean?" Anna's eyes narrowed.

"Violent. That I would grow up like he was. Violent." The word had a hard sound to it. *Violent*. It suggested

163

knuckles and kicking feet; the crack of a slap and blood trickling from the nose. Lou looked down at her lap, the skin around her eyes feeling like sandpaper.

"No, no. Not violent. Not you, love." Anna put the cigarette down and put her arms around Lou. "That kind of thing, that temper, that cruelty, it doesn't pass on from father to child. Course it doesn't. Your dad was like that because he was unhappy with his life. Maybe it was me. Maybe it was the army. I don't know. He wanted someone to blame, someone weaker than him. He took it out on me. That's what violent husbands are – unhappy men and they take it out on their wives."

Lou's head was buried in Anna's chest. She could smell the faint scent of nicotine.

"I kept it from you because I didn't want you to grow up ashamed or fearful. I wanted you, at least for a while, to think good things about your dad. That's why I kept all these things. I always planned to tell you when you were older. When you would be able to live with the truth."

Anna got up from the settee and went across to the cardboard box. With her hands she lifted the photos and letters and put them on to the table. Then she pulled out a piece of paper from the very bottom of the box. She handed it to Lou. On it was an address: *14 Riverside Gardens, Breasley, Exeter.*

"The army gave me that when I phoned up to see if he still lived at the base. That's where he lived two years ago when he came after us at the fair. You can do what you like with that. I don't mind if you contact him. I'm not running away any more. This is where I'm staying."

Anna picked up the cups and took them out of the room.

Lou looked at the piece of paper for a long time. After a while the words began to blur and she closed her eyes to stop the tears coming.

Later, after Lou had held the paper for a while, she got up and went across to the table where the photos and letters were. She replaced them in the box, neatly, with great care, so that she'd be able to read them all later. Then she put the box on the floor and picked up the matches from the coffee table. With trembling fingers she laid the piece of paper with her dad's address in the ashtray.

It had to go. Because some day, in spite of herself, she might be tempted to look up a map book and find the area. She might even be drawn towards it, taking an unfamiliar bus or train, walking along a strange street, looking from door to door to spy the right number. She might even walk up a pathway, ring on a bell, wait until a man stood there saying, *"Yes? Can I help?"*

That's why she couldn't keep it.

She struck the match and let the flame dance in the air. After a few seconds it died away so she struck another, cupping her hand round it protectively. She held it there until the heat began to singe her skin, so she blew it out. In the back of her head she could hear Anna in the kitchen, knives and forks clattering together, drawers opening and closing.

She lit another and held it over the paper, centimetres away. She watched it until it looked like a wall of flame in front of her eyes. She blew it out in a panic and stood looking at the piece of paper lying doggedly in the ashtray.

Disneyland. It had been a dream of hers. To walk round the giant funfair holding her dad's hand – a man in a soldier's uniform, a war hero, someone who had sacrificed his own life to save others. That's why they'd never gone to Disneyland.

The sound of funfair rides came into her head and she remembered standing with Anna up against the wall of the ghost train, listening to the fake screams of the people inside, her real father only metres away from her, a man in a long mac, looking for them, chasing after them.

She snatched up the piece of paper and put it in the box with the photos and letters. She should destroy it but she couldn't. It had to stay.

Without saying anything she tiptoed along to her bedroom and lay down in the dark, hugging the box in her arms.

After what seemed like a long time Anna came in and lay down on the bed, her knees gently behind Lou's, her face in Lou's hair, her arm across Lou's waist. The two of them, on the single bed, lying in spoons.

TWENTY-ONE

It was the end of October, the last day of the half-term holiday.

The three of them were sitting in the living room of the flat. There were packing cases everywhere. Ruth and Anna were cross-legged on the floor. Lou was sitting up on the settee. Tommy was asleep in the bedroom.

They were playing a game. If You Won The Lottery. What would be the first ten things you would buy?

"A house in France," Ruth said, her shoulders rising in glee.

"A luxury yacht," Anna said.

"A new stereo," Lou said.

"A car."

"A shop."

"Designer clothes."

After some quiet thinking time, Ruth said, "This is ridiculous. We'll never win the lottery. We don't even buy the tickets!"

"No, silly," Anna said, her fingers getting lost in Ruth's hair. "That's not the point, is it, Lou? It's not meant to be *real*. It's like a psychological massage, giving the mind something pleasurable to think about."

Lou raised her eyebrows. Her mum was always using long words these days. That and reading bits from different books out loud. Plus they'd started to buy two newspapers every day, and various magazines.

Ruth stretched her arms up to the ceiling. "Did you tell Lou about our new neighbours?"

"Yes," Anna said. "You remember, Lou, that tall thin man and his tiny wife. On the right-hand side, number sixty-two. The ones who recycle everything." She had a handful of her own hair and was winding it round and round her two fingers.

Lou smiled. Mr and Mrs Friends of The Earth, her mum had called them.

Then there were the neighbours on the other side. Ruth had told her about them. "These two old ladies, Lou, with the most beautiful Persian cats! They sit high up on the back brick wall, pale blue, looking inscrutable."

"The cats, I take it, not the old ladies," Anna had butted in.

"Silly!"

Lou had laughed, imagining two round ladies in blue perched on a high wall.

The new house.

All four of them were moving into it the next day. She had her own bedroom and so did Tommy. Anna and Ruth would share.

"*Do you feel all right about that?*" Anna had said a dozen times.

Lou had nodded rapidly, but inside she was full of confusion. Anna and Ruth together, like a husband and wife. It made her feel odd, awkward, *embarrassed*. When girls in school asked her about her home life she didn't mention it. It was secret and she intended to keep it that way.

The four of them were like a family, though, she had to admit that. Ruth was kind and nice and Anna was happy all the time, singing and smiling a lot, talking about decorating and new settees and beds.

"Are you my sister?" Tommy had said one day, laboriously cleaning his own glasses.

"You should be so lucky," Lou answered. But when they went to the shops together she let him put his sticky hand into hers and she was willing to stop at the park so that he could have a go on the swings.

One day, in the middle of September, she'd been leaning against the climbing frame while he'd been whooshing back and forth, and she'd seen Charlie's van pull up. She'd turned away immediately, afraid that he would see her, embarrassed about what she would say. When she turned back a few minutes later the van had gone. Even though she hadn't wanted to see him, to face him, she'd felt a flood of disappointment through her skin.

Later, when everything was packed and she was cleaning her teeth, Anna came up behind her and said, "Last night in this old place."

"Yes," Lou said brightly, her mouth full of foam.

"It'll be all right, you'll see," said Anna.

"I know," Lou said.

"Look." Anna showed her a packet of twenty cigarettes,

unwrapped. "I bought these to put them on the mantelpiece, in the new house."

Lou smiled.

"This time we'll settle, Lou, I promise."

This time they would settle.

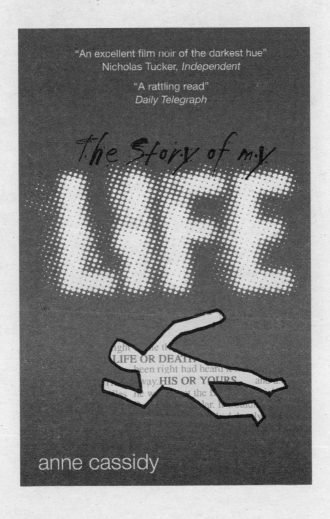

From the award-winning author of LOOKING FOR JJ

GIRL LOST

anne cassidy

A child has been stolen...